PLAN 9 FROM OUTER SPACE

(BASED ON THE 1957 FILM BY EDWARD D. WOOD JR.)

JARED MICHAEL DELANEY

Cover Art by Nickolas Jackson

@cinetrediciart

Print ISBN - 978-1-968357-12-2

For Nate and Luc.
Who knows what you'll find?

Okay. Here's what happened.

In 1945 (as time is reckoned on Earth) the human race set off
some bombs.

Big ones.

Annnnnnnnnd…some *other* types of people noticed.

You know.

Up there.

It kinda went like this:

Somewhere on an interplanetary observation platform, Space Station 7.

ALIEN 1: (*watching a monitor screen*) Did you see that?
ALIEN 2: (*not looking up from his phone*) See what?
ALIEN 1: That flash! Shockwaves! A ball of atomic fire!
ALIEN 2: I dunno.
ALIEN 1: We should tell someone!
ALIEN 2: (*walking away while texting*) Yup. I'll get right on that.
Alien 1 rushes out of the room, panicked and sweating.
…Way more than you'd think.

Here's what happened next.

The intergalactic throne room.

ALIEN 1: (*rushing in, shaking and shivering. It's a bit much, to be honest.*) Sire! Sire! Sire!

ALIEN KING: (*idly scrolling his phone, not even looking up*) You know what's weird about that? "Sire"?

ALIEN 1: There's been a—

ALIEN KING: "Sire" means "dad," essentially. So when everyone is calling you "Dad," it's, like… disconcerting. Which is a great word, by the way. I should use it more often.

ALIEN 1: (*confused, but rolling with it*) The humans have discovered atomic energy! They've *weaponized* it!

ALIEN KING: I don't want to be everybody's dad. That gets exhausting. And expensive. And *disconcerting,*

ALIEN 1: This could threaten the entire galaxy!

ALIEN KING: …I mean, being "Daddy" would be fine. Know what I'm saying?

ALIEN 1: YOUR MAJESTY!

ALIEN KING: (*finally looking up from his phone, startled*) Yo! Volume!

ALIEN 1: (*bowing hastily*) Apologies, Your Majesty. But there's a threat! To our very existence!

ALIEN KING: (*sighing heavily*) Okay. What do you want me to do about it?

ALIEN 1: Permit me to engage our safety protocol plans immediately to see which is most effective!

ALIEN KING: (*rolling his eyes and turning his attention back to his phone*) Fine. Yes. As long as it's not here with me.

(*Alien 1 bows again and hustles out as the king offers a dismissive wave.*)

Back at that platform.

Alien 1 bursts in (kinda like the Kool-Aid Man)

Alien 2 nearly falls over, what with the surprise and all.

ALIEN 1: I've gotten permission to engage safety protocols!

ALIEN 2: What?

Alien 1 breaks open one of those red-folder-type things, you know the kind.

Those things they're always snapping open, in, like, a submarine movie for the launch codes.

A look of triumphant glee sets across his face.

Alien 2 looks at him like he's crazy.

ALIEN 1: At long last! It's time! Time for—

PLAN ONE
BUREACRACY

For most intelligent species in the galaxy, confounding rules and regulations had been avoided or discarded eons ago. They can become an impenetrable wall of paperwork, signatures in triplicate, and files, files, files.

The Klezmers, who look surprisingly like humans, having developed a simplified program of institutional oversight, assumed that by creating such cul-de-sacs of crippling exactitude, they would be able to stop humanity's weapons development dead in its tracks.

They were deeply, deeply wrong.

By sending in carefully-chosen double-agents, the Klezmers were able to penetrate the highest levels of human governance. Using that influence, they mucked up the works, creating an endless stream of bureaucratic nonsense before approval can be given to *anything*, let alone weapons systems.

But—to their shock and dismay—humans *embraced the* logjam of it all, finding pleasure in granting and denying every small request or command, using endless reams of paper for every form not properly filled out, and putting stamps that marked requests as 'Approved" or "Denied."

In other words…they loved it.

It slowed weapons development down, but humankind didn't abandon it.

~~PLAN ONE~~

It was time to move on to...

PLAN TWO

PARANOIA

IT HAD LONG BEEN ESTABLISHED through observation and study that the human race was particularly susceptible to paranoid thoughts and conspiracies. Basically all you had to do was have a whisper campaign promoting whatever theory you wanted and humanity would find a way to embrace, amplify, and disseminate said theory, throwing all kinds of monkey wrenches into all kinds of works.

(Not that the Klezmers knew what monkeys were. Or wrenches, for that matter.)

With that in mind, the Klezmers put into motion a plan to create and stimulate public tensions, obstructions, and objections to new atomic energy programming. They spread word of increased planetary violence, the potential harm from food and water contamination, the monetary cost of such endeavors and the lasting impact such weapons would have on future generations.

That should have ground humans' plans to a halt!

But...

Yeah. No dice.

That kind of talk, rather counter-intuitively, made humans even *more* sure that this kind of defense program was the only way to go.

Plan Two took root, but not with the desired effect.

~~PLAN ONE~~
~~PLAN TWO~~

No matter. The Klezmers switched gears to—

PLAN THREE

MUTUALLY ASSURED
DESTRUCTION

THE KLEZMERS FELT like Plan Three was a winner.

Using their secret agents, they ensured that all nuclear powers and rivals on Earth would match each other's level of development at roughly the same time. In other words, no one nation would have a clear advantage over the other.

So, if someone launched an atomic missile, one would come right back at them!

Seemed like a no-brainer. Who'd want to ensure the destruction, not only of their native country, but of their species as a whole?

Right?

Wrong.

That was a hard *"no."*

There were folks on either side of the conflict who were *convinced* that their nation would not only *win* said atomic war but would *thrive* in the aftermath.

…What can you do about that kind of insanity?

Not that I'm judging.

…Much.

~~**PLAN ONE**~~
~~**PLAN TWO**~~
~~**PLAN THREE**~~

Time to slide over to—

PLAN FOUR
AUTOMATION

THE KLEZMERS WERE *FEELING* it on this one.

Using subtle bits of info-dropping and carefully-placed industry insiders, they managed to improve humanity's capacity for construction and assembly. In other words, they put machines in place, particularly in the military-industrial complex that was rapidly rising around the globe.

The thinking was—when humans saw how automation would further erode mankind's ability to regulate its own weapons' systems—that jobs and safety and security would be *sacrificed* in the name of commerce and convenience. They would abandon such automation and return to perhaps... well...maybe not *agrarian*, per se, but something that would be more easily manageable from the Klezmer point-of-view.

Yeah, that was *not* what happened.

To the Klezmers' shock, they watched humans *embrace* the decomposition of their own agency and willingly submit themselves to the continued side-lining of themselves in the history of their own journey.

~~PLAN ONE~~
~~PLAN TWO~~
~~PLAN THREE~~
~~PLAN FOUR~~

Back to the drawing board.

Which, in this case, meant—

PLAN FIVE

MORALITY

OKAY, so this was a time-honored classic:

Appealing to the better angels of humanity's nature.

(Not that the Klezmers believed in *angels* exactly, but they *did* have a weird thing for sculptures made from dental floss. I know, I don't get it either. But what can I tell you? They were nuts for dental hygiene, apparently.)

The Klezmers helped fuel a global anti-atomic movement, starting with humanity's youth.

They're generally the quicker to see the consequences of potentially destructive forces, regardless of species. Maybe it's because they're likely to be around longer. Who knows?

The problem with this strategy was that the youth were often *dismissed* out of hand by the ruling class, who had too much invested in the finances of annihilation. That proved to be the case here on Earth too.

Dismissed as cranks and kooks and other words that start with a hard /k/ sound, the anti-atomic movement was buried before it even was born.

Another failure.

~~PLAN ONE~~
~~PLAN TWO~~
~~PLAN THREE~~
~~PLAN FOUR~~
~~PLAN FIVE~~

This was getting serious.

The Klezmers rolled up their sleeves, took a deep breath, and took another swing.

This time with—

PLAN SIX

THE SPACE RACE

I won't sugarcoat it.

This one was *risky* for the Klezmers.

If they aided humanity in reaching the stars, generations before they were estimated to be ready for such a thing, it could dramatically backfire. Humanity could become a threat even *sooner*, wreaking havoc throughout the known galaxy.

However, the hope was that by entering a far more expansive collective of life, mankind's capacity for wisdom would grow (there had been evidence of this result with other species in the past).

By seeing they weren't alone, the idea was humanity would see that building weapons of devastation were not the way forward. That extended hands outwards was the better path. That they could too take a place among the vast cosmos, a welcome addition to the assembly of lifeforms.

I know I'm a broken record here, but that's not how it went down. The problem, in a nutshell, was the word "race."

A species as naturally competitive as humanity wasn't so into growing & learning. They were into *winning*.

At all costs.

That' was what happened as the Klezmers nudged rocket technology around the Earth forward. The various human nation-states were all about gritting their teeth and beating the other guy.

In other words, nothing had really changed.

<del>PLAN ONE</del>
<del>PLAN TWO</del>
<del>PLAN THREE</del>
<del>PLAN FOUR</del>
<del>PLAN FIVE</del>
<del>PLAN SIX</del>

Faaaaaaantastic.

All good. No problem. Still had a few plans left.

Like—

PLAN SEVEN
ENTERTAINMENT

"BREAD AND CIRCUSES," the Romans used to say.

That was how you kept the people in line. Distracting them with stories and spectacle, while making sure they're well-fed.

Along the way, maybe throw in some subtle hints and lessons about the dangers of going too far.

Humans really seemed to dig these things called "movies."

The Klezmers didn't have prerecorded visual entertainment. Again, there was this whole thing with the dental floss and staring at reflections in those tiny little tooth mirrors.

So they were into this! Investing cash earned from the other plans that had failed, the Klezmers produced low-budget films about the dangers of atomic energy, with monsters, creatures, aliens, and robots.

(Most of those designs were based on some friends of the Klezmers, FYI.)

They figured if they could *teach through storytelling,* humans would get this was a *bad idea* to keep building these missiles and bombs.

After all, who wanted evil masterminds and super-tall

ladies knocking down skyscrapers and murdering thousands?

Yeah.

Turns out *everyone* wants that.

They want it all the time!

Mankind didn't give a damn about whatever subliminal messaging the Klezmers were putting out there. They just wanted the show.

Bread and circuses.

~~PLAN ONE~~

~~PLAN TWO~~

~~PLAN THREE~~

~~PLAN FOUR~~

~~PLAN FIVE~~

~~PLAN SIX~~

~~PLAN SEVEN~~

Things were getting a little *tight*.

It was time for—

PLAN EIGHT

A DIRECT APPEAL

A SELECT GROUP WAS CHOSEN.

Twelve brave Klezmer souls.

Sent on what could be a suicide mission to reveal their existence to the people of Earth and to convince them of the folly of continued expansion of nuclear technologies and atomic weaponry.

In an effort to prove less threatening or startling, native Klezmer musical instruments were brought along as well, music long known as the universal language.

If these Klezmer heroes could disarm the humans with their charm and music, then surely they'd be more willing to listen to reason and scientific fact.

The plan seemed foolproof.

Something not taken into account would be the effect that *mankind* had on the Klezmer mission.

Upon landing on Earth, the Klezmers went into populated areas, playing their native music, in an effort to show they weren't a threat.

And I'm here to tell you…it was a *hit*.

The group, known as "The Klezmer Twelve," were getting bookings all over the place: Weddings, birthdays, anniversaries, you name it.

They got a talent agent faster than you can say "Nuclear Apocalypse," and soon they were playing the circuit up and down the east coast of the United States. The Klezmer explorers soon found they *liked* it on Earth.

A lot.

Last the Klezmer Cosmic Empire had heard of them, they had disappeared into some place known only as—

"The Catskills."

~~PLAN ONE~~
~~PLAN TWO~~
~~PLAN THREE~~
~~PLAN FOUR~~
~~PLAN FIVE~~
~~PLAN SIX~~
~~PLAN SEVEN~~
~~PLAN EIGHT~~

Well.

Now… there was only *one* plan left to the Klezmers.

One plan remaining to stop humanity from not only threatening their own existence, but life throughout the galaxy on the whole.

The Klezmers feared it.

With all their hearts, they feared it.

It was a technology difficult to control with terrifying moral and physical consequences.

Shocking. Stupefying.

It involved the resurrection of the dead and the use of weapons so advanced, but yet so precise, as to seem like magic.

But there was nothing else for it.

The Klezmers could not see another way forward.

It had come to this.

The final plan.

The plan that had *never* been used, but whose legend spread terror throughout the known inhabited universe.

The Klezmers knew that if they did this, if they involved this final plan, there was no coming back. Everything would change.

Everywhere.

They girded their loins and threw back their hair and screwed their courage to the sticking place (which wasn't where you'd think it would be) and cracked open—

PLAN 9 FROM OUTER SPACE

By Jared Michael Delaney

(Based on the 1957 film written and directed by Edward D. Wood Jr.)

CHAPTER
ONE

"LET ME ASK YOU SOMETHING," Hugh said softly, the funeral taking place just a few feet from them.

His fellow groundskeeper at the cemetery, Jay, was nearly asleep leaning on his shovel.

Hugh gave him a hard push and Jay fell forward like a drunk playwright on opening night, face hitting the dirt.

"Ow! Dammit! What was that?"

"I said I had a question," Hugh replied, still trying to maintain some respect for the service. Some of the mourners had looked over in their direction.

Jay picked himself up with disgust.

"Well? What?"

Hugh looked carefully around and then lowered his voice even further.

"You ever seen someone dressed like that? For real, I mean?"

He gestured to the coffin resting atop the planks across the open grave. Jay shook his head slowly.

"Ain't never seen nothin' like it. First of all, who dresses like that in *life*, let alone in death. Know what I mean?"

Hugh wasn't entirely sure that he did, but he figured it

was better to go along with it. Jay was rolling now. So it just kept going.

"Dressing like... I dunno, a witch or something, or a vampire or some kind of creature feature. Ask me? That's some Communist-type shit."

The political component wasn't one that Hugh was expecting.

"What?"

Jay rolled his eyes at his younger (and decidedly stupider) friend.

"Think about it! Rasputin?!"

Hugh opened his mouth to speak and then realized he truly had nothing to say.

Jay settled against his shovel again.

"Mark my words, kid. This has the makings of some kind of invasion. Our American way of life will be taken away, right under our noses, just like that!" He snapped, loudly, earning some admonishing looks from those gathered.

"Oops. Sorry, folks," Jay said quietly, tipping his hat.

"I don't get it. What does communism have to do with a lady dressing like she's in *The Wizard of Oz* or something?" Hugh asked, genuinely confused.

Jay shook his head, pity emanating from him in waves.

"It must be nice. To live in your head, Hugh. So quiet all the time. No noise."

"That feels like you don't really mean it when you say that, Jay."

Sighing, Jay turned back to the little service, nearly wrapped up.

"How she'd die?" Hugh said. "Do they even know?"

Jay shrugged and closed his eyes.

"I heard it was something about spoiled ham on a hot day."

"Spoiled ham??"

"SHH!" came a swift rebuke from the guests. Hugh held up his hand in apology.

It was over, finally. The mourners gathered shook hands, offered hugs, and then drifted away, a bit at a time.

Hugh and Jay waited patiently. The husband of the dead woman was the last to leave, of course. He threw a handful of dirt on the grave and then shuffled off himself.

After he was out of earshot, Hugh turned back to Jay, even as they both began shoveling dirt back into the grave.

"Why's he dressed like he's going to the opera?"

"How the hell should I know? Keep your mind on your shovel. Sooner we get this done the sooner I can get out of here and get over to bowling night."

Hugh's ears picked up at the sound of that.

"Bowling? You're going bowling?"

Jay just kept on shoveling

"I like bowling."

No one has ever shoveled like Jay shoveled.

"Could I come bowling? I'm a good bowler. Got my own shoes and everything," Hugh said, as hopeful as a virgin on prom night.

Jay sighed again. The sound of the condemned. But he had no one to blame but himself.

"Yes, fine. You can come bowling. Now will you help me cover this up? Otherwise she'll get up and start walking around, for Christ's sake!"

Hugh joyfully pitched in, throwing dirt around like it was his job. Which it was.

As engrossed as they both were, with visions of strikes, spares and cold beers in their heads, neither of them noticed the flash of light in the distance beyond the trees.

CHAPTER
TWO

"Let me ask you something," said Danny the co-pilot while the commercial airplane banked slowly over New Mexico as it arced its way towards Los Angeles.

Captain Jeff Trent, chief pilot of this flight, didn't respond right away. Instead, he reflected on a question of identity. It occurred to him, just now, in this very moment, that in over two hundred hours of flight time, he had never learned Danny's last name.

Would it be rude to ask now? Probably, right? Especially given all those late nights in strange cities and strange hotels. You'd think he would've heard it *somewhere*. Or even on a name tag.

Jeff stole a quick sideways glance at Danny's uniform.

The badge on his jacket simply read:

Danny.

Dammit.

He was just going to have to bite the bullet and ask.

But not today.

"What's on your mind, Danny?" he responded cheerfully, not betraying a hint of the internal struggle within him.

He hoped.

"Why is it 'New' Mexico? Why didn't they call it...I

dunno…anything else? Or even 'Mexico II'? I mean, I've *been* through New Mexico. It doesn't look new. Not a lick of it."

Jeff chuckled to himself.

Same ol' Danny.

"That's a great question, Danny. I'm glad you asked. I don't have an answer, but you can be sure I'm going to be thinking about it. For a long, long time."

Danny sat back in his co-pilot's chair, a satisfied smile on his face. Just the response he had been looking for.

The plane's radio crackled to life.

"Burbank Tower to American Flight 812, Burbank Tower to American 812…come in. Over."

Jeff grabbed the com.

"This is American 812, Burbank. Over."

"Just checking in on your ETA."

"On schedule, Burbank. Smooth sailing so far. Over."

Danny laughed to himself.

"What's up, Danny?" Jeff asked brightly.

"Just thinking, you know…what are the odds?"

"The odds of what?"

"That the tower operator at Burbank would be *named* Burbank. First of all, I don't think Burbank is that common a name. I can't recall ever meeting a Burbank before. Can you, Jeff?" Danny asked, with the seriousness of a pope.

Jeff honestly didn't know how to reply to that. He *hadn't* ever met a Burbank.

"Great point, Danny."

"Thanks, boss," Danny replied, as satisfied as golden retriever pulling a duck from a pond.

The cockpit curtain slid open, and Edie, flight stewardess, slid in with a grin on her face.

"Captain. Danny. How we doing up here? Need anything? Fresh coffee?"

An expression of true confusion crossed Danny's face.

"Fish coffee? What the heck is that?"

Edie opened her mouth to reply, but Danny got there first.

"Are you saying it's *made* from fish? Ohhhhh, wait! It's the scales, isn't it? Using the scales to *filter* the coffee! Man, what an idea that is, and really makes perfect sense when you think about it. I mean, those scales are designed to sluice through the water, to keep debris and dirt and whatever out of the internal systems of a fish, so why *wouldn't* they be perfect for making coffee? I gotta hand it to you, Edie. I don't know if you've considered marketing this product, but I think it's a million-dollar grab bag! Every diner in the country will want this! Plus, you know, keep the fish for filets and stuff!"

Danny shook his head to himself with a rueful smile. He was nailing it today.

And he knew it.

There was a silence then.

Edie looked to Jeff, who slowly shook his head 'no.'

"Anyway," Edie continued, "let me know if there's anything you need."

"How are the passengers, Edie?" Jeff asked.

She shrugged. "Most of them are asleep now. I imagine they won't be waking up until we land."

"Good," Jeff replied. "We're almost home."

"Captain, do you think that—"

But before Edie could finish her thought, there was a loud *BOOM* and a tremendous flash of light, nearly blinding them all. Jeff grappled with the flight stick, the plane rollicking a touch as he blinked his vision back to normal.

"Holy cow!" Danny exclaimed. "What was that??"

Jeff looked out the port side window and, frankly couldn't believe what he saw:

A silver disc, large, spinning in place, with blinking lights flashing in sequence. It had a bulge rising out of its center, with what looked like windows or portholes.

"Oh. My. God," Jeff said softly to himself. "Get a load of this!"

Danny and Edie crammed themselves to the pilot's side to take a look. It was a little close for comfort, as far as Jeff was concerned. The three of them hadn't been packed so tightly together since that layover in Providence.

What a morning *that* had been.

But Edie's gasp snapped him out of the reverie. She gripped Jeff's shoulder tightly and he was reminded of how strong she was.

Man, those bruises were *never* gonna fade.

"Captain! Is that…is that…a…a…"

"A FLYING SAUCER!" Danny shouted. "They're real! They're here!"

"What do we do? What do we do?" Edie exclaimed, fear running through her voice, just like it had that night when Jeff and Danny had insisted that *they* wear the masks this time.

"Easy now, team," Jeff said, hoping his voice was as calm as he was trying to make it. He had no idea how to handle this. He had served in the Marine Corps during World War II, but he had spent most of that time undercover as a chorus girl in Paris.

That was an entirely different kind of combat.

He reached for the radio to alert the tower, but before he could do anything, the saucer vanished in streaks of light and sound, like it had never been there.

As the plane hummed gently through the air, the three members of the flight crew were quiet, trying to process what they had just witnessed.

Just then, the com system sparked to life, making all of them nearly jump out of their skins.

"American Flight 812, this is Burbank Tower. Radar has you nearly home. Anything to report? All copacetic on your end? Over."

Danny, Edie, and Jeff exchanged looks. They truly had no idea what to say.

Just like that night in Muskogee with the ball gags.

CHAPTER
THREE

WHAT NEITHER JEFF NOR DANNY, Edie, nor Jay and Hugh for that matter, realized in that moment, was that the world was about to irrevocably change.

Likely forever.

…Which is what 'irrevocably' means. Sorry to be redundant there. Back to it.

The very saucer that had buzzed past Flight 812, its lights spinning and flashing slowly, touched down gently in the middle of the cemetery outside of Burbank, California.

Conspicuously, it was not far removed from a fresh grave, one wherein a recently deceased woman, dressed all in black, lay for her eternal rest.

There was a humming then, low and deep, followed by a mechanical beep.

A silver arm extended from the saucer, an emitter of some kind on its end, along with two claws. It reached out towards the grave and pointed down.

The humming grew louder and there was a sudden burst of white light from the emitter, so fast it was as if it never happened. The claws extended, hovering a moment over the grave, and then they *plunged* down.

Pulling up slowly, they had the corpse of the dead woman, wife of the old man, within their grasp.

But by the ankle. Upside down.

Trying to pull her up, the claws' grip slackened and she plopped down into the overturned earth with a thud.

All good. Let's go again.

The claws repositioned themselves; down they went. This time they picked her up by the head. Probably not as uncomfortable as it looked, right?

They inched slowly, slowly, slowly, towards the saucer proper...she was almost there...there was an open basket waiting for her, and....

Nope.

Slipped out again. Crumpled like a rag doll.

Rub the hands together. Clap it out. Got this!

The claws reached down, this time around the waist (this *had* to be a winner, this time, didn't it?) But the arm started jerking, a little violently, and the corpse woman swung wildly from side to side.

...Seemed as though there was a teensy disagreement on how best to operate the saucer arm. The basket extended and the arm, now settled, moved so...very...gently...and...

DROPPED THE BODY RIGHT IN THERE!

The arm retracted swiftly, retreating back into the depths of the saucer. The basket, meanwhile, rotated into a vertical position, as if the body was now standing upright.

There was another low humming and flash of light. As if in response, the woman's fingernails grew exponentially, becoming long and sharp, almost like talons.

...Except the nail polish she had on (black, obviously) didn't extend with them. So they were pretty patchy-looking, frankly.

And then—something horrible happened—her eyes opened! Ebony and deep, like midnight pools of oil.

The now-hideous Ghoul Woman raised her arms and shuffled out of the basket, marching her way through the cemetery that was to be her home for eternity and now was her personal garden of murder!

Hugh and Jay were winding their way back to their truck, shovels in hand. And Hugh simply could not shut up about bowling.

"Swear to God, Jay—I'm a strike machine! I whip that ball down there and it bounces off the rails and BLAM! Right into the pins, and they go zipping every which way!"

He smiled and swelled with pride so much he was practically glowing.

But Jay stopped dead in his tracks.

"Hold on a second, Hugh. Are you tell me… are you telling me that you use the guard rails? On the gutters? The ones that kids use?"

Hugh nodded enthusiastically.

"You bet I do! I mean, that's why those rails are there, right?"

Jay closed his eyes and sagged at the waist.

"That's not how we play, Hugh! Not in *my* bowling league! That's for *children!*"

"Yeah, but…I mean…wouldn't it be easier if you *did?*" Hugh responded, as hopeful and innocent as a spring lamb.

Jay was considering how best to slaughter such a lamb when a hissing sound surrounded them, like air escaping a tire.

Whirling around, they were astonished to find the woman they had just buried standing before them, looking as fit as a fiddle, honestly. Her arms were outstretched, hands like claws, reaching for them with menace.

"What in Sam Hill?" Jay said, backing up and tripping, ass over teakettle, to the ground.

"Who's Sam Hill?" Hugh asked earnestly. It was the last thing he ever said, as the dead woman, whom he couldn't believe chose to put to rest in such an outfit, ripped his throat out with malevolent glee and then turned to Jay.

He scrambled backwards and promptly fell.

There was nowhere to go. Nowhere to run.

This was the end.

Well, Jay thought before his own heart was torn from his chest, *at least I don't have to take him bowling now.*

CHAPTER FOUR

T HE OLD WIDOWER stepped outside of his home and immediately tripped.

He righted himself straight away, hoping that no one saw him.

So when he heard the laughter, he presumed that the two small boys across the street, sitting on their bicycles, pointing and laughing, were thinking of something else.

Which was, obviously, the only explanation.

…Right?

It had been *rough* since his wife had died mysteriously. He had told her, repeatedly, that week-old, "sun-dried" ham sandwiches with mayo were not an Eastern European cuisine. But, headstrong as always, she wolfed it down, like she'd never eaten before.

He was pretty sure she did it just to raise his hackles. And he wasn't even positive he knew what hackles *were*.

In the end, blame didn't matter. She was gone.

And he had *no* idea where anything in the house was. Not the tea. The laundry detergent.

The cat.

That thing was *long* gone. Sometimes, at night, he thought he could hear a faint meowing somewhere in the deep distance, but honestly, who the hell knew? It was entirely possible there had never been a cat. She had always told him that they had one, but he never saw it. Nor any cat food or cat boxes or anything that was cat-related.

No doubt another one of her schemes designed to drive him mad.

She was contrarian to the core. But that's why he loved her. The challenge. The arguments. The slapping (of him by her). She also insisted on wearing the most form-fitting dresses money could buy.

…Actually he didn't mind that so much…

Regardless, she was gone. The house was empty without her. So much so, that he couldn't bear to be in there for too long. Hence stepping outside. Some fresh air would do him good, he figured, even though living so near the airport created a level of air quality that had been officially labeled as "non-human."

Bah! Bureaucrats! he thought, even as he coughed violently as soon as he stepped out.

The coughing fit grew severe, which made the boys laugh harder, which made the old man furious, which made him move deliberately in their direction…which made him trip *again*, over the ivy vines and flowers that his now-dead wife had *insisted* on planting, despite his protestations.

I'm allergic! he would cry to her, fist raised in a pouting rage.

She would dismiss his concerns with a wave and a swish of her witchy hips.

You'll get over it.

And now here he was, having face-planted on his own front stoop, while being mocked by children on bicycles.

Well. He'd show *them*.

First, he'd punch them. Right square in the nose. Ten-year olds *should* be punched. Not that he could muster much force. He quite literally could no longer gather the strength to pick one of those dreaded flowers. Tough little bastards. Anyway, the punch wouldn't do much damage, but that wasn't really the point.

Maybe their little brat eyes would water. Hope springs eternal.

Next, he'd steal their bikes and sell them on the black market. Truthfully, he didn't really understand what the black market was, how much money he could get or how to get there, but he was fairly certain that was the plan he should take.

While in the midst of this reverie, the widower stepped into the street.

As the boys watched with eyes as wide as those of giant squids, a truck (flower delivery — how's that for irony?) came *hurtling* down the block like a Saturn V rocket and sent that old man flying into the air.

For the briefest of moments, he thought:

I'm free!

It was probably the happiest he'd ever been in the entirety of his life.

Then he hit the ground.

Which was... how to say it...?

Less good.

CHAPTER
FIVE

NEVER HAD SO many of the same people been in the same cemetery in so short span of time. Really, it was some kind of a record.

Adding further oddness to the proceedings, the old man had stipulated he be buried in whatever he was found dead in. Apparently, it was a cost-saving measure.

So, in the casket he went, cloak, tux, the whole nine yards. (And it very nearly *was* a full nine yards. That cloak had a *lot* of fabric to it.)

He was laid to rest inside a crypt, rather than in a plot next to his wife. According to rumor, this was *also* a cost-saving measure, the rationale of such the gathered mourners enjoyed debating.

A bit loudly.

"How could you say a thing like that?" one such mourner exclaimed, dressed in black with a smart hat on. She was a neighbor of the now-deceased couple, and had always found them to be pleasant enough, if a bit distant and a bit strange. "That's just awful."

"Look, I'm just telling you what I heard," her companion said, wearing a dark suit and tie. He had a more-intimate knowledge of what went on in the neighborhood, with all the dirt of the community at his fingertips. Quite literally.

He was the trash collector.

"I know that the *official* story is something about family tradition, women returning to the earth, men preserving knowledge of the future or some such," he pontificated with assurance of a person who knows what toilet paper families prefer to use. "But the word is, they were flat broke! I don't think he worked at all, do you?"

She shrugged, shaking her head.

"I never saw him do much except...you know...*lurk*."

The trashman nodded his agreement as the pair walked slowly away from the tomb into the growing mist.

"*Lurking*. That's it exactly. He was a *lurker*."

"And as for her..." she said, lowering her voice, looking around to make sure no one was nearby, but not so low that no one could hear.

...Because what would be the point of that?

"...I've been told, with those *outfits* of hers...that she might have had a special...clientele? *If* you know what I mean."

The trashman did indeed know. He has always suspected that the dead wife had a whole other life- -as a fortune teller.

"Should've taken advantage of that when I could've," he mused out loud.

"*What*?" she said, absolutely scandalized.

He held up his hands in innocent protest.

"Hey, don't pretend like *you* wouldn't want to try it, just once. Everyone is curious about stuff like that."

"Excuse me, I don't think that you have any idea what I'm—"

But she stumbled. And then she screamed.

They had come across Hugh and Jay.

What was left of them anyway.

Inspector Daniel Clay was tired.

Dead tired.

End-of-the-world tired.

And he was set to wrap up his career. Tonight was his final shift, but in the middle of his farewell party, the call came in:

Dead bodies in the graveyard.

Which, to Clay, didn't seem too remarkable. After all, the whole joint was full of dead bodies. Wasn't that the point of the place? Dead body storage?

His captain had strode through the carousing cops, a grim look on his face, getting right in Clay's face, which was covered in confetti and lipstick stains.

"Whaddya say, Clay?"

"Retired, Cap. In a little less than an hour," Clay responded with firmness.

"Excellent. Then for that amount of time, you're still on the clock. And we got some dead folks over in the cemetery across town."

"Sounds right, Cap," Clay said, smearing the frosting from his cake across his face as he stuffed it into his mouth. There was a roar of laughter from his fellow cops.

"ZIP IT," the captain shouted, "Or you'll be writing parking tickets in tutus until I say otherwise!"

That didn't do much to quiet the squad, all known to be avid fans of the local ballet.

"Cap, what do you want from me?" Clay asked.

"Two of the groundskeepers were found, torn to pieces, by all accounts. You're gonna head down there, right this damn second, and find out what the hell is happening. Is that clear, Inspector?"

Clay hurled his cake against the precinct wall where it

landed perfectly in position with all the *other* pieces of cake that had already been tossed there.

"Fine, Captain. I'll do it. But just remember," Clay said, leaning in with menace, "that's *my* cake on the wall. And it had better still be there when I get back."

The captain clapped him on the shoulder.

"You bet it will, Inspector."

He watched as Clay stormed out of the precinct, a few other officers going with him. The captain shook his head.

"That's a hell of a cop," he said. "Now clean that cake up."

Now in the cemetery, Clay talked with his lieutenant; Harper was his name.

"Harp," Clay intoned, his voice a gravelly pit, "tell me what happened here."'

"Can't say as I can say, Inspector," Harper responded.

He was a little confused as to why Clay was the one giving orders. For one thing, he was retiring in something like thirty-eight minutes. And for another, lieutenants outranked inspectors.

No time for that now. There was a murder to solve.

"There was a funeral earlier this evening. And after the burial service, a couple of folks found these two, just as you see 'em. All ripped up, like."

"What do the lab boys say?" Clay asked, looking at the murdered groundskeepers with narrowed eyes.

The gathered cops all exchanged glances.

"They're all at the lab, Inspector," Harper said.

Clay nodded with dramatic intent.

"Just as I suspected. You all stay here. Stay busy. Find me some details that will seal this case tighter than a whiskey barrel."

Harper nodded, still not clear why he was taking orders.

"Sure thing, Clay. What are you gonna do?"

"I'm going to search this cemetery. Up and down, tooth and nail, thick and thin, until I find out what happened here."

"You sure you want to go alone?"

"Of course," Clay said, shrugging off the concern. "What could happen? I'm retiring today."

CHAPTER SIX

It HAD all made perfect sense at the time. Jeff and his wife, Paula, had bought the house near the cemetery for a number of reasons:

First—it was dirt cheap. The house had been on the market for a good, long while after the original owner died. In the house. And potential home-buyers were put off the deal for that reason.

Jeff couldn't understand that.

Sure, the owner died in a horrific ritualistic murder that included Satanic symbols carved into the walls with blood (not easy to get out: Jeff could attest to that first hand.), an apparent goat-sacrifice (goat was *delicious*. In his chorus girl days, Jeff had eaten more than his fair share of goat.), and finally, there was supposedly a "poltergeist" in the attic, banging around and moving things. Well, Jeff never went up there. So what did he care about an upstairs tenant who, most of the time, didn't make a sound?

So when the house was still on the market for an absolute steal, it was a no-brainer.

Second—the house (and the cemetery) were incredibly close to the airport. In a pinch, Jeff could *walk* there if he had to. Not that Jeff *walked* anywhere, mind you. What was he? A Neanderthal? C'mon, now.

Third—and this was a big one for Paula—it was quiet. Except for the planes flying overhead. But otherwise? There were no neighbors. No traffic. No solicitors knocking on the door at all hours of the night. Not that Paula minded them, exactly. Especially if they were selling linoleum. She couldn't get enough of it. (It was a problem, honestly.)

But Paula needed the quiet because she was generally not a good sleeper. She'd toss and turn, flailing her arms like a baby albatross learning to fly.

She'd slapped Jeff more than once in the dead of the night. And, to be sure, Jeff *enjoyed* it, but those slaps could cause some damage. Tough to explain the bruises on the domestic flights. Especially when Edie could tell they weren't *hers*.

Regardless of Jeff's whining about "appearances," Paula really had needed to get a decent night's sleep. Jeff didn't understand, because she *could* just be resting all day, after cooking, cleaning and prepping for him to return, of course. Instead she insisted on working on all these "special projects."

Oh you'd better believe Jeff had asked about them, but Paula would just smile and pat his cheek.

"Classified, dear. Strictly need to know."

Jeff would shake his head.

Wasn't that just like a woman?

So, she and Jeff had put an offer in on the house, and it was accepted right away. They moved in and soon found that the house of their dreams was...

...dull as dirt.

Nothing happened.

Ever.

No parties. No potlucks. No neighborhood kids knocking on the door at Halloween (not that Paula celebrated Halloween. Something fishy about that holiday, if you asked her.)

They were boooooooorrrrrrrrrrreeeeeddddd.

So when the police sirens ROARED right past their house after Jeff got home from work as they sat outside with some cocktails (Paula's fourth of the night. No need for Jeff to know that.), Paula was both scared and thrilled.

"Jeff! Oh my, Jeff! Did you hear that? Did you *see* that? What's happening?" Paula asked, her voice trembling with excitement, eyes aglow with something besides adrenaline.

Not that Jeff spotted any of that. He was lost in thought.

Thoughts about flying saucers.

"Dammit, Jeff," Paula said, smacking him on the arm to break his reverie. "Pay attention to me, would you please? Don't make me get the cattle prod."'

Tempting as that was, Jeff knew he didn't have the recovery time built in. He was back on the job soon.

"Sorry, dear. Just can't stop thinking about what we saw tonight. Me, Danny, and Edie."

Paula slammed her drink down on the patio table with disgust.

"If I have to hear about the ropes and the vaseline one more time, Jeffery, I swear to all that's holy—"

Jeff shook his head.

"No, no, nothing like that. Not tonight, anyway. It was something I saw, up in the sky, something that will be with me all the rest of my days."

All right, Paula thought, *let's get to the good stuff* and slammed back the rest of her drink.

"Let's hear it then. Out with it."

Jeff took a deep breath, a deep drink, and looked his wife deep in the face.

"Flying saucers. Over the desert and headed this way. They could be here over us right now, for all I know."

Paula's mouth fell open. Usually something ended up in there when she did that, but not tonight. Tonight was something else entirely.

"Flying saucers? You mean… *aliens*? From another planet?" she asked breathlessly, eyes wide.

He nodded, as serious as the grave. Which was fitting considering that graves were just beyond their picket fence.

"You bet it was, diddly-scumptious," he replied, using his long-held nickname for her, acquired after a long night in the candy factory.

It got gooey in there.

"There were three of them," he continued, suddenly craving sugar. "They buzzed the plane as we were coming into Burbank, so really, not so far away. They zipped past, creating a flash of light and turbulence to beat the band, knocking us all over like cue balls."

Paula snickered.

"Danny must've liked that. Sicko."

Jeff pointed at his wife in positive affirmation.

"In any event, I think they could be dangerous. And what's more, I think that the public should *know* about this. Visitors from another world? Planning to do who knows what all to the human race?"

Paula moved closer to the man that she loved and put a hand on his arm.

"Then why not let them know, Jeff? You've exposed yourself to the public before," she said, a hint of joy in her voice at the memory.

"You're not wrong, pumpkin lips," Jeff answered, remembering that night in the pumpkin patch and the five-dollar bet that followed. "But there's something else to consider."

"What's that?"

Jeff sighed heavily.

"Word came down from the top. No less than the Army is putting pressure on the airline and my crew to keep our collective mouth shut about what we saw. And I gotta tell you, that doesn't sit too well with me."

Paula had never been more proud of her husband than now.

And also that night on Smith Island when he did that thing with the hot butter and crabber's traps. She was *sure* no one on Earth had ever managed to pull something like that off before.

Paula sat down in her man's lap, wrapping her arms around his neck affectionately and kissed him on the cheek.

"We'll figure it out together. We always do. Like the party when we couldn't find the key to the padlock? Remember that? And the boiling point was thiiiiis close? All those people watching?"

He smiled at the memory. Boy, had his face been red. For more than one reason.

He nuzzled into his wife's neck.

"Thanks, darlin," he said, and she leaned down to give him a kiss...

And they were both blown off their seats by a tremendous rush of wind and light, blinding them as they fell.

"Good jumping Jesus!" Paula exclaimed, climbing back to her feet. "What the hell was that?"

But Jeff was still on the ground, staring up at the sky, eyes wide in wonder and fear.

Like the first time he saw the studded leather mask.

"It's the saucers," he said. "They're here."

CHAPTER
SEVEN

After it had cruised past the Trent home, the saucer made its way toward the cemetery; its lights blinking, its engines roaring, its saucerness… saucering.

It was searching for something. But to the naked eye, it would've been unclear as to what. Mostly because the damn thing was flashing its searchlight every which way.

Seriously, it was like one of those strobes where they issue warnings about the possibility of seizures beforehand.

However, the light finally settled, fixing on a singular point. At long last, it had found what it was looking for:

A gravesite. A stone mausoleum. The very same wherein the old widower was entombed.

As the saucer hovered above, the light shifted colors from white to red to green, bathing the entire structure, not just with light but with sound: A deep, low humming.

The beam from the ship pulsed, almost like a heartbeat, or a good dance song, thrumming for a few moments.

Deep within the mausoleum, the body of the old man stirred, hands flexing and knuckles cracking. (But actually cracking because he had been dead and none of those joints were properly 'oiled up' so to speak. So every snap, crackle, and pop was literal. It wasn't pretty.)

He rose from his tomb, swept his legs out, promptly got tangled in his cape, and fell face first on the stone floor with a dull thud, several teeth scattering like dice in a craps game.

A dreadful groan emanated from the reanimated corpse's mouth. It sounded pretty annoyed, truth be told.

Back in the sky, the ship (likely using its remote scanners) had determined it had accomplished whatever it set out to do, and zipped across the cemetery towards the spot where the groundskeepers had been found.

The assembled police were *still* there, searching for clues connected to the brutal murders of the groundskeepers. But due to budget cuts, the forensics department couldn't actually do much, besides hunch over, look at the ground, and say things like '*Seems... inconclusive.*'

It wasn't ideal.

While the cops tried to look busy in case someone spotted them, the spacecraft came zooming past, creating a terrible wind in its wake, powerful enough to knock everyone down like bowling pins.

It was chaotic. Not in a fun "Keystone-Cops" kinda way, but more like in a "This-Is-Our-Tax-Dollars-At-Work?" kinda way.

Hats went flying, bodies went flying, curses went flying. Everything not tied down was up in the air and then hit the deck *hard*. And for Burbank cops, where the most strenuous thing on their agenda was fishing drunk movie stars out of their custom in-ground pools, it proved a real test of their mettle.

And they were found wanting.

If Clay had been there when this happened, first of all, he wouldn't have gone down like that. It was a little-known fact, but Clay was the All-County Standing Up Straight Champion, five years running. The man had balance for days and wouldn't have been swayed on the deck of the Titanic as it went under. Secondly, his gruff demeanor and near-incomprehensible style of speaking left everyone slightly afraid. They would've done everything they could've to keep their feet to avoid a shaming rebuke at the hands of Inspector Clay.

But... Clay *wasn't* there. He was still out in the thick of this graveyard, looking for something, anything, to help him solve these strange murders on his last day on the job.

He wanted to get home as soon as possible. He was baking a slow-rising flan. He had put it in the oven before he left for his shift and it would collapse if he didn't get back to it soon.

He loved a good flan.

Didn't everyone?

So among the tombstones he trudged, heavy-footed and sour-faced, like a sumo wrestler sucking on a lemon.

The sheer *size* of this place was daunting. The cemetery may have had the largest acreage in all of Burbank, bigger than the airport, even, which was just a ways down the road.

Clay was getting frustrated. He hated unsolved puzzles, and his flan was waiting.

So far, this hadn't turned out to be much of a retirement party.

He stumbled his way past a unusually large mausoleum, marble and stone, a heavy iron door as its entrance. So distracted was Clay by his own search, he never noticed that door creaked open slowly and a taloned hand slid out. He never noticed the door slipping free, falling heavily *onto* that hand, causing something inside to yelp in sharp, clumsy pain, retreat back inside, and then push frustratedly against it, forcing it open again.

It was the old widower, risen from the grave for a terrible, hidden purpose, commanded by forces beyond human understanding.

Also, it just *stank* in there. The dude needed some air.

Creeping out, the old man moved silently through the underbrush of the cemetery, (which was impressive, considering how much of a klutz he was). And even though he was the resurrected dead, he still had some sense of propriety. After knocking out so many of his teeth from the spill he took, he held his cloak up to cover the lower half of his face.

Just seemed like the right thing to do, you know?

But Clay *didn't* know. He didn't know any of this. Completely unaware, mind on flans, dog-racing, and Veronica Lake movies (in that order), he stomped his way through the cemetery looking for something to crack the case wide open.

Lost in thought as he was, he never noticed the tall, lithe figure of the Ghoul Woman, just inches from him. Maybe it was the dark of the night. Maybe it was her black dress. Maybe it was a general dismissal of anything not baking-related. Regardless, when she appeared in front of of him, hands like claws, bloodthirsty look on her face, Clay realized he might just have misunderstood the situation he was investigating.

Turning to run, he found his path back blocked by the creature's mate, a man dressed like he was going to a Victorian ball, cape over his face like he was the Phantom of the goddamn Opera.

Clay didn't need to be told twice. Shoot first, let God sort 'em out, right? Pulling out his service revolver, he fired off some rounds, first at the Ghoul Woman, then at the Dark Opera Man. But to no avail. It was as if the bullets made no impact on them at all.

Likely that was because Clay was a terrible shot. No, but really. He once *missed* the broad side of a barn, but managed to hit the bell around the neck of a cow. (He claimed at the time that was what he meant to do, but no one believed it.)

But even if had managed to strike his pursuers, it's doubtful they would have much impact. After all, what were bullets against something that was dead?

And that was the final thought Clay had as the hellish beasts fell upon him.

Well…that and his beloved flan.
Who would ever eat it now?
So sad.

CHAPTER
EIGHT

"HEY, let me ask you something, Lieutenant," Officer Kelton said, with curious innocence.

Harper braced himself. He knew what was coming before Kelton uttered another word.

"What is it, Kelton?" Harper replied gruffly.

"Well. You're the lieutenant, right?"

Oh, Christ, he thought. *This kid was gonna drag it out.*

"Yeah. And?"

Kelton scratched his head underneath his uniform cap. Those things were *itchy*. Mostly because they were made from wool. And hadn't been cleaned in twenty years. 'Budgets' being the reason given by the captain.

"Well, I was just wondering, and I don't mean to get your bee in a bonnet and all—not that I've ever seen a bee in a bonnet. Why would a bee do that? You know? Like… what's the point? Does the bonnet have a flower on it? And *that's* the confusion? I guess maybe I could see that. If I was a bee and all. But still—"

"OFFICER KELTON!" Harper barked.

"Yes, sir?" Kelton said, emerging from the strange cul-de-sac of his own mind. "What's up?"

Harper sighed heavily.

"You were going to ask me something."

Kelton tipped his hat back slightly, with a look of childlike bemusement on his face.

"Huh. Was I? Well, don't that beat all? Can't think of it now, Lieutenant. Ain't that a thing? I'm sure it wasn't important."

Harper was *quite* sure it wasn't important, but he didn't want to encourage the conversation to go on further than it had to.

"How we doing on finding some clues as to what the hell happened here?" he asked with intent. He'd love to have something to report to Clay when he got back from his nocturnal ambulation.

(Harper had been reading his thesaurus lately, and feeling pretty proud of that, thank you very much.)

Kelton opened his mouth to answer when a series of gunshots echoed out through the cemetery, as loud as thunder.

Well. Maybe not *that* loud.

More like firecrackers.

The cheap kind.

"What the hell was that?" Harper exclaimed. "Men, let's *move!*"

He raced off into the depth of the graveyard, the various patrolmen and officers following closely behind. Harper just hoped that someone had marked the location because he had a *terrible* sense of direction. Really, it was just awful. Couldn't find his way out of a wet paper bag.

But that was a problem for another time! Clay must've fired those shots. Harper was damned if he was going to handle the paperwork if Clay turned up dead or missing or caught *in flagrante delicto*.

Harper wasn't sure what that meant, but it sounded delicious.

After running towards the sound for what seemed like whole seconds, Harper and his men found Clay.

Dead.

"Ahhh, son of a bitch," Harper said in a low tone. "Just minutes from retirement and all."

"Geez-louise, Lieutenant," Kelton said, fully scratching at his scalp now. *Could be there some kind of parasite in those hats as well?*, he thought. "Is that the inspector?"

"Sure is, Kelton. And it's a real shame."

Another cop, Larry (that was his last name. Oddly, his first name was Larry as well. Not 'Lawrence.' Just 'Larry.' Officer Larry Larry. Harper shook his head in wonder. He *wished* he had a name as exotic as that growing up. Must've really helped him stand out), rushed up to Harper excitedly.

"Lieutenant, there's a bunch of shell casings all over the place, but I can't tell what Clay was firing at, or even if he hit anything."

"That's good work, Officer Larry. Gather all those casings, and we'll hold onto 'em."

Larry and Kelton exchanged a look.

"Uh, Lieutenant? Why would we do that?" Kelton asked.

Harper rolled his eyes. These kids. Didn't know a damn thing.

"For Christmas tree garlands, Kelton! Christ, stop being such a rookie, would ya?"

"Right, sir. Sorry about that. Don't know what's wrong with me."

Harper sighed. Kelton was all right. Just a little dumb. But weren't they all? The real question wasn't what was wrong with *him*, it was what was wrong with *Clay*. There wasn't a mark on him; no blood, no nothing. If it had been the same situation as those two groundskeepers, he'd be all ripped to shreds. Not so here.

So what the hell happened?

"Larry," he barked. Larry Larry appeared, a little put out

that Harper had used his first name like that if he was telling the truth.

"Yeah, Lieutenant?"

"Let's get Clay bagged up and outta here on the double. Coroner will want to take a look before we turn around and bring him right back."

Another look between Kelton and Larry.

"Why are we bringing him back? And why so fast?" Larry asked.

Harper looked around, not sure if he was supposed to share this information. But, to hell with it. Clay was dead and didn't have any family.

"Well," Harper began, feeling suddenly uneasy. Might be the situation. Might have been the burrito he had earlier. Eel had sounded good at the time, but now…

"Clay had this thing. He told me that when he died, whenever it would happen, he didn't want to be above ground too long. Wanted to get under the earth as soon as possible."

"Why would he want that, Lieutenant?" Kelton asked, genuinely confused.

"Well, it turns out our good Inspector Clay had some… body art… that he'd rather people didn't find out about. Could cause some postmortem embarrassment."

It was the third time around for Kelton and Larry exchanging looks. Frankly, it was getting a little intense.

"Wow," Larry said. "Wouldn't have expected that."

"Me neither," Kelton chimed in. "No place for body shaming, right? Be who you are, that's what I say. Freak flags flying, and all of that."

Harper didn't know what to make of this conversation, but that wasn't unusual for him.

"Zip it, the two of you. You've got your orders. Get Clay out of here and let's process him and get him turned around, right quick. You hear me?"

The two officers snapped a salute and got moving.

Harper stepped away to be alone for a moment. This had all been too much. He needed sometime to process what happened to his friend and superior officer (even though, by the letter of the law, he shouldn't have been). Clay was gone. And now he was in charge. It was a *lot* to handle.

Plus... that eel was making itself known.

CHAPTER
NINE

FOR MOST OF the residents of greater Los Angeles, this was happening in a vacuum.

They were blessedly ignorant of what was transpiring in the Burbank Cemetery and it's surrounding environs.

People went to work. People made movies. People ate corn-dogs (a staggering amount of corn dogs). They drove their cars, they took their kids to school.

In other words, all was normal. An average day in the City of Angels.

Except for two remarkable things that happened:

First—it was announced that the Brooklyn Dodgers were going to be uprooting from the East Coast and moving to LA. To say this set the city alight with excitement would be putting it mildly. The Dodgers! On the West Coast! It was the stuff of American Dreams!

Well—not for Brooklynites, who were devastated by the news and carried the grudge generationally, actually evolving in such a way that the resentment of the moving of a Major League franchise became *embedded* within the DNA of their children and children's children and so on down the line. One would assume they'd get over it as the years passed, but nope. They held on to that bitterness *tightly*, like a sick kid refusing his medicine.

But for Angelinos, this was Christmas morning. A seismic shift in the way they collectively thought and felt about their hometown. That day… it was all anyone could talk about.

Which is unfortunate.

Because the *second* remarkable thing, that wasn't as much noted at the time, was that the city found itself the epicenter for a host of UFO sightings, all across the region.

Three saucers, moving more or less in tandem (maybe *less*), buzzed their way across the skyline—from the Capitol Records Building to the Griffith Observatory, from the Santa Monica Pier to Grauman's Chinese Theatre.

They zipped their way through the air, just above the city, circling, flying, lights blazing, the whole bit.

But…almost no one noticed. Because of the goddamn Dodgers.

One woman, on her way to pick up more diapers for her dogs (who, oddly, didn't need them) spotted the ships. She pulled over and hopped into a phone booth to report it to the police. But when the police dispatch answered, she kept rambling on about the price of said diapers and never got to the UFO part of the call.

They hung up.

A drunk stumbled out of a bar into the day, the sunlight absolutely blasting his retinas. He had the whiskey bottle still in his hand and when he heard the whistle of the saucers as they soared past, he nearly dropped it. He bent at the knees and made a stunning catch of the bottle just before it shattered into a thousand pieces. When he looked back up, he *just* caught a glimpse of the ships as they zoomed away.

Huh, he thought, *they kinda look like baseballs* (NOTE: They didn't). *They're going all out on this Dodgers thing.* And he stumbled back into the bar, none the wiser.

There was a cub reporter at the *Hollywood Chronicle* who *did* properly see the ships in the skies above the city. Thinking he had the story of the century, he raced back to his typewriter.

Truth was, the kid wasn't much of a reporter. But he was an utterly remarkable typist. He could type so fast it was as if you couldn't see his fingers moving. It was a blur of motion and rapid tic-tacking of the keys.

Rushing out the copy and desperate to make an impression, the reporter burst his way into the editing bay, insisting his story be run in a special edition to be distributed right away.

He was met with indifference and more than a little annoyance.

That's when things got serious.

The cub reporter pulled out a gun (except it wasn't real. It was a Roy Rogers toy pistol he had painted black with shoe polish) and held the entire production team hostage until they did what he wanted.

Sighing, the team reset the typeface and printed out a rush edition of the paper, with the headline screaming SAUCERS SEEN OVER HOLLYWOOD. Scrambling to get it out to the populace, the kid loaded up his own truck with the edition and threw it out all over the place for the citizenry to read.

But almost everyone in town exclusively read the *Los Angeles Times* and the only story there was, again, about the Dodgers. So the Chronicle's headline was missed by most. Also, that cub reporter was promptly fired. He gave up his dreams of breaking big stories, informing the world and changing society.

But he *did* get a job as a batboy for the new Dodgers organization and the benefits weren't too bad. Although he got cracked in the head with a couple of fouls balls that left him no longer able to type.

But he figured it came with the territory.

In Washington DC, however, things were a bit different. First of all, the Washington Senators were absolutely terrible. They nearly lost 100 games that season and finished with the lowest attendance of any team in the big leagues. There were rumors that the Griffith family, who owned the ball club, were making efforts to move the team to Minneapolis, of all places.

For Senators fans at large, the response was two-fold: One was "take 'em." The other was "Where?"

So the populace of the city wasn't too distracted by the fortunes of their major league franchise.

Thus it was when the saucers crested across the continent from LA and headed to the nation's capital, most folks in town *did* see them.

And, as a result, there was a bit more alarm at the saucers' presence.

That's when a new player on our stage steps into frame:

Colonel Tom Edwards (formerly of the Pentagon) had been placed in charge of national defense in case of UFO attack. And he was *more* than ready to go when the saucers appeared.

With a rapid deployment so swift it made people wonder why the IRS didn't move as quickly, Edwards got his teams ready.

And as the alien spacecraft made a tour over the Capitol Building, the Washington Monument and the White House, he launched everything he had at the bastards.

"Take 'em down!" he barked into his walkie. That's all that needed to be said.

Rockets launched, bullets flew, bombs exploded. It was a bombardment that would've taken out virtually any other enemy combatant.

But as for the saucers? Didn't do a damn thing.

Everything bounced off, like handballs off a hand…wall.

Clearly, the ships had shielding that protected them from any kind of assault.

Edwards was frustrated and frightened.

And in trouble.

For one thing, he (inadvisedly) did all of this in the skies above the nation's capital, with all that debris coming down on the National Mall and knocking down every single cherry blossom tree.

He was going to have to pay for that.

So much for that fishing boat.

Then, for *another* thing, he had a kink in his neck from staring up at the ships. And it hurt like a son-of-a-bitch.

That was going to be more money down the drain, this time for the special massages he semi-regularly received, which involved several copies of *Encyclopedia Britannica*, linseed oil, and a foreboding German woman named Oogla.

It was in the midst of this financial reverie that his second-in-command, Captain Reynolds, approached his commanding officer gently.

"Sir?"

"Yes, Captain?" Edwards said, still staring up at the sky.

"Sir, no reports of damage to the spacecraft. In fact, they took off without any delay of any kind at all. Also, we're getting calls from the White House, sir. Apparently, we chipped quite a bit of paint off the facade, and we also knocked down the Washington Monument."

Edwards nodded solemnly.

"Yes, that's right, Captain. We've known about these things for a good long while now. But the Army keeps its secrets, yes it does."

"That's great, sir, but about the Monument—"

"Hahahah, no, I don't know any more about them than *you*, Captain. Their motives are as mysterious as ours must be to ants."

"Sir, I've got the Joint Chiefs on the horn and they're *hopping* mad about this—"

"No, that's right, Captain, believe it or not. You think about it. What's to say they haven't been the cause of everything that's come our way as a species? Every tornado. Every flood. Every bastard hurricane. Every damned typhoon."

"Hurricanes and typhoons are the same thing, sir. Only difference is one is from the Atlantic, one's from the Pacific."

"You said it, Captain. We *tried* to communicate with them, radio waves, morse code, hell, I heard that even balloon animals were used once. But those alien sons-of-bitches popped every balloon. Merciless."

Captain Reynolds truly couldn't make heads nor tails of this conversation.

"Sir, the joint chiefs? The President? They want to know what the hell happened out here," he said, trying desperately to keep his colonel's attention.

"That'll be all, Captain. You can report back that the situation is nominal."

"It's not, sir. It's really not."

"Thank you, Captain."

Edwards went silent then, still staring at the sky. In fact, he hadn't made eye contact with Reynolds that entire time.

Reynolds thought about saying something, but then figured it wasn't his place.

Plus, he had Senators tickets that night.

CHAPTER
TEN

HARPER STOOD SLIGHTLY APART as Inspector Clay was laid to rest in the grave picked out by the department. He shook his head at the sight of it.

Didn't seem right.

Nondescript.

Nothing to signify that an officer of the law was interred at this post. But no matter what Harper thought, there wasn't anything to be done about it. Clay, strangely, hadn't left a will – at least not one anyone could find that *wasn't* a paper towel with writing in ketchup.

Clay was well known for his fondness for ketchup. Some would say enthusiasm. Others might use the word *obsession*. Harper figured that a man's relationship with his condiments was not only private, but sacred. He wasn't about to judge such behavior.

Speaking of judges, there wasn't one in the land that would recognize the legal authority of a document written in ketchup.

(Apparently, one judge had said if it had been mustard, there wouldn't been a case, but *c'est le vie*.)

Regardless, with no clear guidance and with the paper towel in question having been used to wipe up a spill, there was no recourse but for the powers that be to put Clay where they felt fit. And since this particular cemetery was getting quite a run of bad press, the brass was more than willing to offer the police department a deal on the lot, as long as the cemetery could then advertise that *their* graveyard was *the* graveyard of choice for the cops. The department went for it. And Harper had to agree. Who'd pass up that offer?

Night had fallen again and as the reverend spoke about the resurrection of the dead and the world to come, Harper was lost in thought.

First of all: Why were all these damn funerals in the middle of the night? Who ever heard of such a thing?

Made no sense.

Second of all: The saucers.

They had soared all over town like birds on the wing and dozens of people had called in reports. Harper couldn't help but wonder if there was a connection between those alien do-dads up there and what was happening *here*, at the boneyard. He tried to remember what he read about aliens as a kid, in the pulps like *Strange Adventures* and *Eerie*. Try as he might, he couldn't remember a damn thing about extra-terrestrials and weird necropsy stuff like this.

(That thesaurus *sure* was coming in handy.)

Third of all: The murdered groundskeepers.

Who would bother to kill, not one, but *both* of them? Could they have been involved in something nefarious? Grave-robbing? Digging up body parts for bizarre experiments and the like?

And what was more—what the hell could have torn two grown men apart like that? There weren't any mountain lions in these parts, certainly not down in Burbank, and the bears were all up in the northern half of the state. Harper supposed that if you pissed off a dog enough, it might do something like that. But it would have to be a *big* dog and almost certainly off the leash.

He couldn't figure it.

And he needed to. Not only for justice's sake, but for his own well-being. After all, one wrong step in this case and he could end up as dead as clay.

Huh. That's funny, he thought.

Dead as Clay.

Dead as clay.

Clay.

"clay."

Harper shook his head. If he wasn't careful, this was a grammatical rabbit hole he would be unlikely to climb out of.

He was known for such things, was ol' Harp.

Best to nip it in the bud now.

As Harper found himself lost in that vocabulary round-about, he was interrupted by Kelton, who came stumbling over with the grace of a baby deer that had been hit by a laundry truck.

"Lieutenant," Kelton said, nearly falling into his superior's arms.

Harper caught him at the last second, holding him up. It was oddly intimate, but in a gravesite filled with mourners, no one looked twice.

"Get a hold of yourself, Officer," Harper scolded. "We've still got plenty of work to do."

"Like avenging Inspector Clay?" Kelton said hopefully.

"Not on your life, Officer," Harper said disgustedly. "We save *that* kind of treatment strictly for unarmed motorists, you know that. Or do you need to brush up on your LAPD rule book?"

Kelton snapped to attention. Time alone with a book was the *last* thing he wanted.

"No, sir," came the swift reply.

There was a groan then, loud and straining, as Clay was lowered into the ground by assembled uniformed and plain-clothes cops. The coffin was big. Had to be, to accommodate Clay's… carriage.

Harper had never talked to Clay about his weight. After

all, Clay dressed well, and his clothes seemed to fit. But there wasn't any bespoke suit in the world that could disguise how much Dan Clay weighed.

The guy was just massive. A bear. In every sense of that word.

...*If* you know what I'm saying.

"If we're not going to– you know– enact our bloody revenge for one of our own, what *are* we gonna do, Lieutenant?"

Harper took a deep breath. He wasn't sure, truth be told, but he'd be damned before he'd say so to Kelton. No chance in hell.

"We're going to finish what Dan Clay started, Officer. We stay out here, search every nook and cranny, turn over every rock and and look under every bush until we find out what the hell happened!"

Harper finished with a flourish, face red, mouth panting a little bit, eyes looking a little... buggy, truth be told.

"Who's with me?" he roared like a lion.

But as Kelton was the only one standing by, it felt... you know... a bit much.

The patrolman raised his hand sheepishly.

"I guess, me?" Kelton said, with all the confidence of a seven-year-old in math class.

"Not as enthusiastic as I'd like, but I'll take it, Kelton. Let's move!"

And with that, Harper... and his new-found sense of responsibility, marched deeper into the cemetery, which had witnessed three funerals in less than thirty-six hours.

What neither Harper, nor Kelton, nor any member of the police force gathered to say goodbye to a colleague (but who had, in the interim, retreated to their respective patrol cars, eating donuts that someone had brought and thus missed everything that Harper and Kelton has said) had spotted was the figure of the Ghoul Woman, dead eyes unblinking, jaws slavering, nails sharpened and ready to tear flesh from bone.

She watched hungrily from the shadows as Clay was lowered into the ground and then, as if being controlled by some outside influence (which, of course, she was), shuffled off into the darkened gloom, with an agenda beyond the understanding of mortal man.

...Or something like that.

CHAPTER
ELEVEN

FAR REMOVED from that Burbank cemetery, the greater city of Los Angeles, the United States and the very Earth itself, a space station hovered out in deep orbit, beyond the reach of radar and radio.

Looking like a hot dog, sort of turned upside down with too big of a bun, the station hummed softly in the vacuum of space. Lights flickered gold and green, just another constellation in a night sky full of them.

The saucers, returning to base after bopping around the globe like Whack-A-Mole moles, slowed their approach and docked, one after the other, with skill and precision.

Well. Mostly.

The third saucer struggled a little bit, bouncing off the docking bay a couple of times before getting it right. Honestly, it did a hell of a job on the paint. Nicked it all up. But that was a problem for another day.

After getting that ship secured, two of the Klezmers, Eros and his trusty first officer, Tanna, disembarked and headed straight for the commander's offices.

Approaching the door, they paused as Eros hit the bell signaling their presence. They waited for someone to answer while Tanna gave Eros a searching look.

"What?" he said finally (and a bit anxiously).

"No, nothing," Tanna replied innocently.

Eros sighed. He knew this was coming.

"Out with it, Tanna. Let's hear it."

"No," she said demurely. "I was just wondering if you thought that—"

"He doesn't care about the finish! The whole station needs a paint job! That's not just on me! The staff needs to be on top of that!" Eros exclaimed a little defensively.

"Take a breath, Eros," Tanna rolled out of her mouth, bored by his worry. "That's not what I was going to say."

"Oh yeah? You weren't going to say… *again*… that I need glasses?"

"Well. I wasn't. And you do. But that's not the point."

Eros couldn't have been more exasperated.

"Then what *is* the point?"

Tanna collected herself. She'd been prepping for this conversation for a while now.

"The point is… are you *sure* this is the way to go?"

Before Eros could answer, the door slid open with metallic efficiency and standing before them was The Ruler.

Now… let's take a second to break down this "title," such as it is.

The Ruler wasn't called "The Ruler" because he ruled anything. That's not to say The Ruler wasn't Eros & Tanna's superior. He was. But that's not why they called him that. They called him "The Ruler" because of an incident that apparently happened a few years back. When The Ruler was… ah… shall we say… *experimenting*… with different "insertive" experiences. Including using a… you guessed it… a ruler.

Rumor was it took two days to get the damn thing out.

He'd been "The Ruler" ever since. He didn't know that, of course. He thought it was a sign of respect. Which, apparently, in some sense, it was. Not easy to get that bad boy all the way up there. Go figure.

"Eros. Tanna," The Ruler stated flatly. "Enter and report."

Walking into The Ruler's office, Tanna was impressed by the barrenness of the space. Nothing on the walls. Nothing on the desk. It occurred to her that the reason for that could be to avoid further penetrative temptation. But who knows? Maybe everything that could be up there was up there already.

"Ruler," Eros began, "So far, all is going according to plan. The humans know nothing of our presence, and we continue to execute our mission without issue."

The Ruler looked at them with a slightly raised eye.

"They know nothing of the Klezmer presence? You're certain?" he asked.

Eros flashed a nervous look to Tanna, who shrugged. She didn't want any piece of this.

"Yes, Ruler. Of course."

"I see."

The Ruler reached into his desk and whipped out the *Hollywood Chronicle*.

"Then how do you explain *this*??" he said, brandishing the paper.

Eros looked to Tanna, who suddenly found the floor very interesting.

"Ah, well. That is… you see, Ruler, that's because—"

But The Ruler slapped the paper down with a dramatic flourish.

"I don't want to hear your lies, Eros. You've exposed yourself!"

Eros whipped around to look at Tanna.

"You said you wouldn't report me coming out of the shower!"

"What?" Tanna said, examining her fingernails.

The Ruler took the paper, rolled it up, and smacked Eros across the face. It didn't hurt. Not exactly. But Eros was a bit fragile.

"Ow!" he cried out, clutching at his cheek as if he'd been shot.

"Oh, relax, Eros. Get it together. Tell me about Plan... what is it? 5?"

Eros and Tanna exchanged a look.

"No, Excellency. We're up to 9, now," Eros said.

"9?" The Ruler exclaimed. "How the hell did that happen? And how much is this costing us, for Klezmer's sake?"

Eros shrugged, like a fourth-grader caught in the locker room.

"Well, I mean..." he stumbled, looking at Tanna, who was suddenly fascinated by the ceiling tile. "Isn't the safety of our people worth any price?"

Sighing like only an exasperated employer can, The Ruler shook his head.

"That's exactly what people who don't have to pay for anything say. I'm telling you right now, Eros, when this is over, I'm checking the books and I'm checking them twice, then likely *thrice*.If I don't find them nice, you're going on ice!"

Tanna chuckled to herself.

The rhyming had started. That's when you knew The Ruler was *really* ticked off.

"Tell me about Plan—?"

"9," Tanna offered.

"9," The Ruler repeated, annoyed.

"Yes, sir..." Eros winced, rubbing his face gingerly. "Plan 9, which involves the reactivation of the dead through shooting electrodes in the pituitary glands of those recently deceased, and thereby controlling them, is working like a charm. We are building an army of zombie slaves!"

Eros raised his fists triumphantly.

Then lowered them quickly as The Ruler stared him down.

"And how large is this army of the dead so far?"

Tanna coughed then, a little dramatically. Eros shot her a look that would've knocked a saucer right out of the sky.

"Only two, your Excellency, but—"

"TWO?!? Eros, how in the name of the Empire are we to take over the planet with an army of two??" The Ruler asked, not unreasonably.

"There *will* be more, Excellency. I promise you that. I ask for your patience as we continue to execute Plan 9!"

The Ruler sat down (softly. He couldn't flop down like he used to. There was a lot of speculation as to why that was).

"I don't know about this, Eros. It doesn't feel like this is a plan that's working. And we're expending a lot of resources, as well as risking serious retaliation from the people of Earth!"

"Trust me," Eros said, leaning forward, hands on desk.

Tanna shook her head. The Ruler didn't like fingerprints on his surfaces. Any of them.

"There's more to come," Eros continued, hoping he sounded as confident as he was pretending. "This is the way to make humanity see! They're making the wrong choices and we are here to correct them, to show the consequences of their actions!"

Tanna had to admit, when Eros got going, she was kinda into it. Too bad there wasn't a ruler nearby…

"Very well, Eros," The Ruler said. "You'll be given more time to prove your point and complete your mission. But mark my words: If you risk further exposure, the wrath of the Klezmers will fall upon you, swift and mercilessly. Is that clear?"

Eros bowed low.

"Yes, sir, your Excellency."

"Good," he said. "Dismissed."

And then The Ruler promptly left his own office.

It was strange.

"Well, Tanna," Eros said, more than a little cockily, "told you it would be fine."

Before she could answer, The Ruler suddenly swept back in, paperwork in his hand.

"Here's the ticket for the paint job on the station, Eros. Learn how to drive the damn thing, would you please?"

The Ruler sighed and exited again.

Tanna turned to Eros, smug as a bug in a rug who had tugged on a mug full of slugs, who needed a hug after being lured to a jug to be used as a drug for a roomful of lugs.

(The Ruler wasn't the only one who enjoyed a rhyme or two.)

"I'm not helping with that," she said.

Eros dismissed her with a wave.

"The fine is nothing. The plan is all that matters, and this one is working!"

"Not really, though. Besides, there's an ethical question here."

Eros scoffed.

"Like what?"

Tanna shook her head dramatically.

"The dead! Using them like this. Don't they deserve the rest that they've earned?"

Eros sighed again.

"First of all, there's no 'deserved.' People are just dead. And that's going to happen to everyone throughout the known cosmos. Everyone dies. It's not a matter of it being deserved. It's just what *is*."

Tanna took a step back, taking Eros in a bit more fully, biting her lower lip.

"How enticingly nihilistic of you, Eros," she purred.

Eros, despite his name, had no game at all and didn't know *how* to handle this.

"Uh... uh—" he stammered, sweat instantly running down his brow like a waterfall.

"Thanks. Tanna."

He smiled awkwardly.

Really awkwardly.

But that just revved Tanna's engines even more.

"Could you... help me... back on the ship, Eros? I left something there. I'm going to need you to locate it for me," she said suggestively as she turned to go.

Eros swallowed hard as Tanna swished away.

He hoped he still had that ruler in the cockpit.

CHAPTER
TWELVE

JEFF FINISHED PACKING the last of his travel items into his overnight bag. He was heading back to work, whether he liked it or not. And he most certainly did not.

There was too much happening, with the saucers and the trouble at the cemetery. It felt like the exact wrong moment to leave. God knows he was worried about Paula and her safety. After all, Jeff mused, she couldn't be expected to protect herself.

Sure, Paula had black belts in krav maga, jujitsu, and a rare and little-seen form of kung fu that required intensive training of the eyelids, but she was *only* a woman.

There's no way she could defend her virtue or the home or anything else. Even though she was a three-time target shooting champion and had advanced degrees in aeronautics and survival training, there was no chance she'd know what to do in the face of a real emergency.

Making a home: Cooking, cleaning—that was what she was *really* good at, even more so than being an internationally ranked grand master at chess and karate (She once won international titles in both of those disciplines at the same time, a feat never attempted before nor since).

Nope, Paula being left alone was a problem, and Jeff

didn't feel good about it at all. But Paula, in that simple way that women had, tried to reassure him it would all be all right.

"Relax, honey," she said to him as he headed for the door. "I'm going to be more than fine. I'm going to spend some time sharpening my katanas and continuing to build my immunity to arsenic and various snake venoms. There's plenty to keep me occupied and distracted from all these horrible things that are happening."

But Jeff wasn't having it, shaking his head with worried concern.

"Baby, I don't want to hear about your womanish hobbies. Something pretty serious is happening, and God only knows how it will shake out! Disaster most likely! And how on Earth could you be expected to handle that on your own?"

Paula nodded, shamefaced.

"You're right, Jeff, of course. Here I was, thinking all of those years learning to hold my breath for more than eight minutes while lowering my heartbeat to just three per hour, all while launching arrows with deadly accuracy at moving targets would be useful in moments just like this. But I'm so glad you were here to remind me how wrong I was."

Jeff smiled ruefully, like a parent at a wayward child.

"I knew you'd understand eventually, honey. Don't get me wrong, it's terribly impressive that you were able to build a combustion engine from scratch in the kitchen but you're still only a woman, and your safety is my primary concern."

She leaned in and kissed him, grateful for his care.

"When you're right, you're right, darling. I'm such a lucky girl to have you. And you know, arranged marriages don't often work out for the best these days."

Jeff chuckled.

"You said it. But your father offered such a good price for you, how could I have possibly passed it up? I'd be leaving money on the table!"

Paula smiled. What a day that had been.

She gave Jeff a playful whack on the arm (that hurt quite a bit. Probably because of the weightlifting she'd been doing).

"I'm going to need you to stay inside, here, where we know it's safe," Jeff implored.

"Even with the various structural instabilities that the house has demonstrated recently?"

Jeff sighed.

Women.

"You told me you were going to fix that, honey," he said, exasperatedly.

Paula quickly became apologetic.

"I know, dear, I know. But the cross-beam construction proved a little trickier than I thought at first glance. I'm still working on the blueprints for the new model."

It never ends, Jeff thought, shaking his head.

"And you think you can be expected to take care of yourself when you can't finish a little home renovation project like this? C'mon, babe."

"You're right again Jeff. When you're right, you're right. And you're *right*," Paula said with rueful shame coloring her tone.

"So it's settled then. You're going to stay here, in the house, waiting for me to return."

She smiled up at him. Paula really did love him, especially as he was so considerate at how incompetent she clearly was. At *so* many things.

"Now get outta here, mister! I need you to bring home that bacon! I'll be waiting for you to get back to me as quickly as you can."

"You got it, doll," Jeff said. "Let me pilot this flight to New Mexico and then I'll turn right around."

"Great," she said enthusiastically. "I'll be ready."

Jeff smiled gently and headed out, confident that Paula would be smart and she wouldn't do anything foolish.

…Like that time she enriched uranium with a coffee filter and avocado peels.

Unbeknownst to either of them, as Jeff left for work and Paula gently closed her front door, a saucer reappeared in the skies over their home, bobbing like a cork in the water.

It found its way to the cemetery, and lowered itself slowly, like a man with sore legs descending on the toilet.

Nestling amongst the tombstones, the mysterious craft hummed and buzzed softly, preparing for the next phase of Plan 9…

Jeff made it to the airport in record time and his flight was already underway and up in the air. He was feeling good.

Paula was safe. And because of the quaaludes he popped before taking off.

Danny appeared suddenly into the cockpit and settled into the co-pilot's seat.

"How's tricks, Jeff?"

"Goddamnit, Danny! You scared a year's growth out of me! Where have you been?"

"What do you mean?" Danny asked, tilting his head like a house-trained puppy.

"What do you mean, 'what do you mean?' Where have you *been*? This flight left Burbank nearly an hour ago, and you were nowhere to be found!"

Danny blushed.

"Oh, come on now, Jeff. Don't make me say it."

"Say what?"

"Well… you know things have been tight for me as of late. Financially and all."

"Yeah." Jeff drawled out. "So?"

Danny turned a deeper shade of red and turned away, shrugging.

"Well. I've been living in the bathroom."

Jeff blinked twice.

"The bathroom? Where?"

"Right here. On the plane. It's tiny, don't get me wrong. But once you settle in, it's not that bad, gotta tell you. And it saves me a ton on rent."

"Hold the phone now, Danny," Jeff said, mimicking holding a phone, just in case Danny didn't get the metaphor (internal visualizations were tough for him), "you're... you're living *in* the airplane's bathroom? How do you sleep?"

Danny's embarrassment turned to strange pride.

"Oh! I'm glad you asked. Here's something you don't know about me. You probably think I sleep standing up. But, since I was raised in the circus and all—"

This was already more information about Danny's home life than Jeff had ever heard.

"—I was trained to fold myself into a little square. Like a napkin. And flatten out. So I just curl into that space between the toilet and floor, and I'm good."

He smiled, a grin to beat the band. Jeff was more perplexed than ever.

"Stop living in the bathroom, Danny. That's an order."

Danny saluted.

"You got it, Captain!"

"I've got plenty of other things on my mind than worrying about your sleeping arrangements, so I'd just as soon not," Jeff said with worry.

"What's up, Jeff? What's on your noggin that's got you weighed down?"

Jeff sighed. He hadn't wanted to bring this up. The last thing he needed was his crew worrying and fretting about what was coming down the pike. But, he needed to talk to *someone* and Danny was, at the bare minimum, someone.

"The saucers, Danny. They're still out there. God only knows what their plans are, but I have fear that they're up to no damn good, no matter what way you slice it."

Danny whistled, low and deep.

"Man. Forget about those bastards. Let me ask you something, Jeff."

Jeff hesitated to respond. Whenever Danny wanted to ask something, it was never good. Interesting, maybe. And occasionally erotic. But never good.

"What is it, Danny?"

"Well," Danny began, tipping back his hat as he eased into his chair, "I've been thinking. About them saucers. How they're a technology we've never seen before. Right? Which must mean they run on a power source that we couldn't possibly comprehend. You would agree with that assessment?"

Truth be told, Jeff was stunned that Danny knew the words 'technology,' 'comprehend,' and 'assessment', so he was already kinda knocked for a loop.

"I'd agree, Danny. Sounds about right to me."

"Okay then," Danny said, feeling the moment. "So here's what I'm considering: That power source. Must be milk, right?"

There was a silence that hung in the air then, like a fog bank on an otherwise clear day.

"What?" Jeff managed.

"Well, you know. Saucers hold milk. So I figured, 'hey, maybe these aliens have figured out a way to make *their* saucers take that milk and turn it into energy! Energy enough to power spaceflight and to transverse the stars! MILK!!!" Danny said triumphantly, raising his hands in glory.

Edie walked in at that moment, and Jeff was never so happy to see her in all his life. And that included that night with the vinyl zip-up bodysuit.

"Hey there, fellas," she said cheerily. "Anyone need coffee or anything else?"

Danny turned to Edie, a smirk on his face.

"Tell you what I could use, Edie: A tall glass of milk and a weekend in Albuquerque. Whattya say?"

Edie smiled, the smile of a woman indulging a child.

"You're sweet, Danny. But no milk. It doesn't keep. And Albuquerque isn't for rookies."

Danny's face fell with shock.

"What do you mean? I'm not a rookie! Remember Colorado Springs?!?"

Leaning down, Edie patted him on the cheek gently, sweetly.

"I *do* remember. Which is why you're still a rookie, kid."

She kissed him lightly, winked at Jeff, and wriggled out of the cockpit.

"Anyway," Jeff said, "I'm worried about Paula, being home alone and all."

Danny looked at Jeff a bit askance.

"What do you mean? Didn't she stop that bank robbery down in Waco all by herself that one time? Took out a crew of thieves and hired muscle by herself, with only a toenail clipper?"

"Sure, sure," Jeff said, frustratedly. "But that was *different*! She's just a woman, Danny."

"Right you are, Captain. If you're so worried about her, radio the tower. They can put in a call, check on her, then report back to you!"

Jeff was so elated by that idea he could've kissed Danny. But not without his frog mask securely on. That was a hard red line.

"Great thinking, Danny! Really well done. I'm going to give that milk idea of yours some real consideration!"

Danny sat back, chuffed. Today was a great day.

Jeff picked up his radio.

Paula was finally settling down for the night. It had been a full day since Jeff left. She had all that woodworking to finish, as well as practicing the piano sonata for the concert she was giving in a couple of weeks. She hoped that Jeff would be able to make it to that one. He hadn't seen any of them yet, saying that classical music was "un-masculine."

She chuckled and shook her head.

That man.

Sitting down on the bed, she was just putting on some cold cream when the phone rang, startling her.

At this hour, it was either Jeff (when he went out with the boys, what trouble they got into), or the FBI (they called when they needed her help to crack a case. Which was more often than not).

In picking up the phone, she was surprised to hear it was the flight control operator from Burbank Tower. She never knew his name, but she sure recognized his breathing. After so many anonymous calls, you get to know one respiratory pattern from the next.

"Hey there, what's going on?" she asked brightly, but secretly hoping the heavy breathing would continue.

She listened for a moment and nodded, laughing.

"Oh, that Jeff. Tell him I'm fine. Really. All is well here and that he needs to keep his head where it is: The clouds!"

She was pretty proud of that line.

"Thanks. No, I appreciate the concern. Have a good night."

With that, Paula hung up the phone and shook her head with a chuckle.

Again.

And thought—

That man.

Again.

So distracted was she by her own bemusement, Paula never heard the door downstairs creak open. Nor did she hear the heavy footsteps clambering up the stairs. Nor the low, ugly moans that came down the hallway towards her bedroom door.

For all of her accomplishments, Paula couldn't hear a damn thing.

Likely because of her time as a howitzer gunner during the war.

Regardless, she didn't clock any of those sounds, nor did she spot the door to her room as it pushed open.

Standing there, draped in his operatic funeral attire, was the dead husband, the Ghoul Man, the mate of the Ghoul Woman (which makes sense). His cape hovering over half of his face, he had come for Paula Trent... for what purpose... well... that was a little unclear. Both to him and to Paula.

She sat on the edge of her bed, looking at him quizzically.

"Now, listen," she said finally, "I know I placed the order for the male... ah... *companion*... but it was supposed to be for Friday night, when my husband would be on a longer overnight flight. He could be back within a couple of hours. And I told your booking agent I need to take my time with the gentlemen callers that come my way. So you're going to need to head on out of here."

The Ghoul Man moaned slightly beneath his cape.

But Paula wasn't having it.

Holding up a hand to silence him, she said "No, no, no. I've been *very* clear. No tips, especially not for arriving on the wrong day and time. So you can beg all you want, but I'm not doing it. And you can be sure I'll be writing a *very* negative review of your services."

And with that, (whether out of mindless instinct or anxiety about a poor rating, none could say), the Ghoul Man leapt across the bed to snatch at Paula, who promptly dodged his clumsy attack.

"My goodness!" she exclaimed, running for the door. "This *wasn't* in the package that I ordered, I'll have you know!"

With that, she sprinted out of the room, down the hall, and raced out of the house with all the speed she could muster. Which was considerable, as she was the state record holder in the twelve-hundred meter.

The Ghoul Man was hot on her heels however, moving far more gracefully than a recently-reanimated corpse should.

Until he got to the stairwell.

That's when he stepped on his own cloak and went ass over teakettle alllllllllllllll the way down to the ground floor.

Staggering to his feet, the Ghoul Man grumbled incoherently.

…But it kinda sounded like "Son-of-a-bitch."

Out into the night he went, pursuing that helpless woman, Paula Trent.

CHAPTER
THIRTEEN

WHILE THIS WAS HAPPENING, the Ghoul Woman, following a directive all her own, shambled her way through the dark cemetery.

She moved unerringly through the mist and gravestones, searching for something.

Well. Hold up.

Not exactly.

First of all, she tripped. A lot. Over roots and stones and things. Part of the problem being she never looked down her own feet, and who can do that, no matter the terrain without taking a spill?

Plus, there were the arms.

They were always outstretched, grasping, clutching at… whatever. And, as a result, more often than not, those limbs would get tangled up in the frankly stunning number of bare and scraggly trees and bushes that were all over the place.

(You know, in retrospect, maybe those two groundskeepers, Hugh and Jay deserved to die. 'Cause this place was a *mess*.)

Anyway—on she went, fitfully finding her way through the graveyard until she came upon a recently overturned burial plot.

The headstone read, in large bold letters, CLAY.

Turning her undead eyes to the disturbed earth, a glow and hum emanated from them, as if she were the conduit for larger forces.

Her unknown and terrible task completed, she turned and shuffled away... falling flat on her face first, but she got right back on that horse, so to speak, and vanished deep into the cemetery grounds.

But what of her dark purpose? What was the result of that?

As if in answer to those very questions, Clay's grave began to rustle and collapse in on itself, loose soil being pushed out to the edges of the plot.

A large, pale hand *burst* through the earth, soon followed by another. Grasping out onto either side, the powerful hands pressed downwards, and from the grave, a bald, round head emerged.

Clay.

His corpse, powerful if unwieldy, was now a plaything for the Klezmers and their nefarious plans.

Rising like a bad moon , Clay clawed capriciously from the corners of his cold, clammy casket. Worms, ants, beetles scurried from his flesh as he rose to his feet like an undead colossus.

He was now a simple engine, used as part of the plan to bring all of humanity to heel.

If there was any part of Clay left that knew what was happening... it remained silent. All that mattered was fulfilling the wishes of his new overlords. And stomping out any resistance to their rule.

But before he could that—

—Dammit, there was something in his shoe. It was *really* annoying. Even for a scientifically-induced zombie.

He stretched forward, trying to reach his feet. But even when he was fully alive, *flexibility* wasn't a word associated with Daniel Clay.

But he didn't give up and kept extending down... down... down... until he ended up rolling like a big, dead, white beach ball down the slope of the cemetery.

Bringing humanity to heel would have to wait a couple of minutes.

Paula ran with gusto, but she couldn't shake the cloak-clad creature creeping up behind her. Every time she turned, he was there. No matter what path she took or what route she chose.

...*Part* of that may have been because—despite her many, many, talents—Paula had virtually no sense of direction. Like... literally none. She also suffered from a very rare visual deficiency: Tree blindness.

Some may have heard of 'facial blindness,' the inability to recognize faces. For Paula Trent, her condition was a version of that. One that never caused her a moment's harm in her life.

Until now.

She couldn't tell one damn tree apart from another.

And she literally ran in circles, at state champion speed, no less, thinking that, at every turn, the Ghoul Man had come upon her anew.

At one point, the Ghoul Man was so struck by her repeated circles that he just stood in place, figuring that, at some point, she'd crash right into him. He may have been dead, but he wasn't dumb. There was enough cunning in there to figure this out.

And to do *The New York Times* crossword.

But not the Saturday edition. That was too hard for anybody.

After her umpteenth lap around the cemetery, with the

Ghoul Man always appearing right on her heels, Paula finally suspected something was wrong. What was more, it occurred to her that if she didn't make a change of some kind, she was going to end up in the arms of this creature. Which, under different circumstances, may have been fun. But today wasn't that day, not by a long shot.

So Paula made a choice: she closed her eyes, sprinting at full speed on whatever path she found herself on at the moment.

Daniel Clay—or in actuality, his hulking reanimated corpse—meanwhile, was compelled to follow an electric impulse, an odd tickling in the back of his zombie brain, and soon, he was also on the trail of Paula Trent.

As he groaned and stumbled his way forward, he was joined by the Ghoul Woman, still tripping over every damn thing, but making a go of it as best she could.

Paula didn't know that. All she knew was that her endurance, up until now a thing of legend, was finally wearing out on her and if she didn't get somewhere safe soon, her days were numbered.

And then, as if on cue, Paula burst from the trees, finding the road that led from town.

It just so happened a car was passing.

Now... in that car was one Farmer Calder. What was odd about ol' Farmer was that "Farmer" was both his profession *and* his first name.

Seriously.

When Farmer was a kid, he dreamed big, like so many people do. He *wanted* nothing more than to become an umpire in the big leagues. He *loved* nothing more than calling strikes and balls. Farmer would often spend hours outside, by himself (there weren't any friends nearby and his parents didn't send him to school), calling imaginary baseball games from behind the plate—which was an actual plate from his mother's kitchen.

When she found that out, he got whupped, but good.

If that sounds sad and lonely... well, that was because it was.

But Farmer didn't care! All that mattered was calling those players safe or out (he preferred calling them 'out,' mostly because Farmer would get *very* dramatic for those calls. Really, it was practically modern dance).

That was when he was happiest.

But Ma and Pa Calder weren't having it. Not for one bit.

One day, when Farmer was out in the fields, replaying the World Series out in his mind, his father came stomping right out onto the baseball diamond that Farmer had cut out of the cow pasture.

"Dad—" Farmer began, but before another word could come out of his mouth, his father smacked the makeshift umpire mask right off his face.

"Boy—what are you doing? You touched or something? Ain't no baseball out here! And stop carving up my land with all those chalk lines you're drawing all over the place! The cows keep licking them and getting sick!"

Farmer turned to look and, yes indeed, the cows were licking at the chalk. And vomiting.

That probably wasn't great, he figured.

Seeing the disappointment on his only son's face, Pa Calder (that was *his* first name. The Calder family had some strange traditions), felt a twinge of regret. After all, he didn't want the boy to live a life of crushed dreams. But he did want him to understand his place in the world.

"Listen, son," Pa said, putting his hands on his boy's shoulders, "I know you're wantin' to be things you ain't. And I don't blame you. But you don't got the sense God gave cornstalks, so you're not going to be—whatever it is you think this is. But you *do* have a calling. And it's an important one, make no mistake. That's why your Ma and me named you Farmer. Because that's what you're *meant* to do, you hear me?"

Farmer had taken all of that in and nodded yes with all the enthusiasm he could muster (which wasn't much). He didn't want to upset his father any further. And he knew that the chances were slim that he would've made it to the big leagues.

So it was the farming life for him. And he had settled into it nicely, for the most part.

Not much happened, and even less changed. But... after his folks were gone, Farmer would go out to that pasture, draw himself a baseball diamond, placing all the cows as if they were position players (he managed it by installing salt licks at the approximate points on the field), and he'd call games to his heart's content.

Folks in the area knew about Farmer and his odd proclivities, but he kept to himself and his milk was excellent (likely because of the salt intake) so people were happy to let him live out his fantasies as he will.

That night, Farmer was driving back from a milk delivery, lost in thought about the vagaries of the rule surrounding catcher's interference, when Paula Trent burst from the tree line and dashed towards the road, collapsing in a heap.

Farmer didn't know the Trents well, but he could occasionally hear sounds... *human sounds, if* you get my meaning... from their property that he couldn't rightly explain. But, as his father taught him, there was a lot beyond his understanding, so let it go.

Paula Trent had always been polite to him and he figured that was the most you could ask from most folks.

Spotting her from his car, he immediately pulled over and rushed out to get her.

"Mrs. Trent? You all right?"

She could barely respond. She seemed all in, and clearly had been running at top speed for some time.

Gathering her in his arms, Farmer took up Mrs. Trent and put her in the car.

If he had stood up and turned around, he would have seen the Ghoul Man was there, lurking out of the woods, lurching his way towards the car.

Now, if'n Farmer *had* seen that, it's likely he wouldn't have thought anything about it, one way or another. Because —truly—Farmer didn't have the sense that God gave corn stalks.

Farmer got into the driver's side and turned the key. Nothing happened.

"Well, shucks," Farmer said quietly, trying again. All the while, undead alien doom was creeping up unawares behind him.

"C'mon now, girl," he muttered and tried his engine again.

Nothing.

The Ghoul Man was nearly there.

"Let's goooooooooo, you little junker!" Farmer said and the engine roared to life, pulling out into the night with alacrity, even as the Ghoul Man reached out his hands for the bumper, exhaust shooting unto his face and dirt kicking up on his beautifully-kept cape.

"Hang tight, Mrs. Trent," Farmer said. "We'll get you set, as quick as strike one, two, three, you're *out!*"

But that last bit was lost on her, as she appeared to be unconscious.

Well, that was fine, Farmer ruminated as he headed towards the Trents' home.

Gave him more time to figure out that catcher's interference.

CHAPTER
FOURTEEN

THE STRANGE LITTLE trio of the undead automatons lumbered mechanically through the unusually large cemetery, heading towards a spot they themselves were unaware of.

But if a wayward traveler happened to follow (although why anyone *would* do such a thing was beyond comprehension), it would have become readily apparent.

There, height rising just slightly over the treetops, metal hull gleaming in the dull, ugly twilight, sat one of the saucers.

How *literally no one else* was able to see this hulking monstrosity of alien engineering could only be accounted for one of two ways:

One—the Klezmers had exceptional cloaking technology, shielding their craft from both prying eyes and the effectiveness of radar.

Which was possible, right? After all, they could traverse through the stars without too much trouble, so it was likely that there was cloaking tech. They had already proven to be so much more advanced than humanity, so likely this was within grasp as well.

Two—and this was looking more like the winner—people were just stupid. And not really able to pull their attention towards anything that didn't immediately concern their little lives in the moment.

Whatever the reason, the massive ship sat unmolested in the vast, dark recesses of the graveyard, waiting to reveal its terrible purpose to the world.

The Ghoul Man and Woman and the zombified Clay lurched into the clearing where the saucer sat patiently.

Approaching the vessel, a metal door appeared from a seamless side of the craft, sliding open. The three creatures made their way in, like kids in line for the roller coaster… or death row inmates marching to their fates.

Deep in an interior cabin of the ship, Tanna watched from a computer monitor. But she was distracted. She was double-screening and her attention was split between the events of the moment and…

A Klezmer cooking show. She couldn't get enough of them. On the screen, a renowned Klezmer chef, a female named Atmos, was describing best ways to prepare "unknown" meats, hot and cold, salted or not, and so forth.

Tanna wasn't sure she was so into that idea. Salt was always an issue for her. High blood pressure and all.

Eros strode into the room.

"Hey," he barked suddenly, causing Tanna to jump like a cat in heat. Not that Klezmers had cats (instead, they had a catlike creature called a *"spormf,"* but really, not worth explaining).

"Eros!' Tanna exclaimed. "You startled me!"

"Aren't you supposed to be monitoring our new agents? Not watching food porn!" Eros said disapprovingly. "You know how I feel about this."

Tanna quietly changed the channel without comment. Word was that Eros and Atmos had a thing back in the day, but then she left him for her supplier of unknown meat.

…That was both a profession *and* a euphemism.

"Apologies, Eros. It won't happen again."

The monitor now only displayed the three beasts as they

made their way through the the ship, now just outside of the chamber Tanna and Eros found themselves in.

"Good," he said, "see that it doesn't. For now, let's do a status check on our agents. Make sure functionality and compliance are all up to snuff."

As if on cue, the door to the compartment glided open, and in shuffled the terrible trio.

Eros pulled something off his belt that looked like a squirt gun (in fact, it *had* squirt gun capability. Planet Klezmer was extraordinarily hot and so it was considered a polite greeting to squirt passers-by with water, to help with the cooling process) and flipped a switch, pointing it at the three undead.

They stopped as one, mouths agape, awaiting commands.

"So cool!" Tanna said excitedly. "Gimme!"

Before Eros could say another word, she snatched the gun from his hand and hit the button. The beasts shuffled forward.

"Red light!" Tanna said, hitting it again, and they stopped dead.

"Tanna."

"Green light!"

They stepped forward.

"Stop it."

"Red light!"

The three stopped, swaying a little bit as they did, struggling to maintain their balance.

"Green light!"

Eros swiped the gun from her hands.

"Would you cut it out, please? You're like a child!"

As he fumbled with the controls on the gun, the undead agents stomped ahead, arms outstretched... *maybe* a little bit pissed that they were being toyed with. Who could say what goes on in the minds of the recently undead?

Regardless, forward they came.

And Eros couldn't turn off the gun.

"Son-of-a-bitch," he muttered, slapping the instrument

like the side of a television. "This damn thing always jams at the exact wrong time."

While he was focused on the controls of the controllers, the creature that was once Detective Daniel Clay lumbered forward, bent on only one thing:

Destruction.

"Eros," Tanna said drily, in faux warning, "watch out."

This would show that uptight prick a thing or two. Don't ever be making Tanna turn off her stories.

Undead Clay was soon upon him, massive hands wrapping around Eros' throat, squeezing with unbelievable strength, causing him to drop the control gun.

"Agh!" Eros sputtered. "T—Tanna… the gun!"

Tanna was suddenly *very* interested in her fingernails. She did really need a mani-pedi sometimes soon. How had she let them go for so long?

"P-puh-please! Tanna!"

The Ghoul Man and Woman, meanwhile, were still lurching ahead themselves, just more slowly than Clay. And when they got a little too close for comfort to Tanna herself, she decided that enough was enough.

Sighing dramatically, Tanna picked up the gun from the deck of the ship.

"Never make me turn off Atmos again, Eros. I don't care about your relationship or hers with the mystery meat, got it?"

Eros nodded. Well, not so much nodded, but more like moved his chin slightly up and down within Clay's powerful grasp.

Tanna pressed the button, sending fresh electrodes into Clay, stopping him cold. His arms went slack, and his hands fell from Eros' neck.

"Well," Tanna said brightly, "I'd say that was a successful test of the equipment, wouldn't you, Eros?"

He glowered at her and switched the monitor back to the cooking show.

CHAPTER
FIFTEEN

LARRY AND KELTON were not pleased.

"I'm not pleased," Kelton said.

"I hear that," Larry said. "These shoes just don't fit."

Kelton stopped dead in his tracks.

"What?"

"You know what I'm talking about. These department-issued shoes. They don't stretch, they don't give. There's no breaking them in. You're just expected to wear them all the time, and it's uncomfortable!"

Larry caught himself with wonder. A fresh thought just occurred to him.

"Holy cow, Kelton," he said, with the same tone of amazement Vasco de Balboa must've used when he discovered the Pacific, "is that why they call cops 'flatfoots'?"

Kelton blinked.

"I'm going to ask two questions."

"Shoot," said Larry, "but not literally!"

He laughed then, a sound like someone breaking a wine bottle over the bow of a ship.

Kelton waited for it to pass.

"Question one: You do know that you don't have to be in uniform all the time, don't you?"

Larry opened his mouth to speak and then promptly closed it.

"Question two: Did you ask for your size? Or just take what they gave you?"

Larry looked down at his feet, looked back up to Kelton, back to his feet again.

"Sizes?" he said finally, a child lost in the woods.

Or—in this instance—the cemetery. The two officers were tasked with searching through the vast graveyard, but for what they weren't quite sure.

"I'll tell you this," Kelton said, avoiding looking at Larry as the poor dolt tried to pry off his shoes, "I don't know what they expect us to find out here. This whole area is enormous. And there hasn't been any evidence of *anything* yet. It's dark and I'm bored."

"Not me," Larry said brightly. "Any day I get assigned to you is a good day."

The sincerity of that statement made Kelton feel badly and simultaneously want to slap Larry across the face with a fish.

A cod, preferably.

Just one good *whaaack*. That would do the trick. And would be *so* satisfying.

"Whatever, Larry," he finally said. "Point is, I don't know what the hell we are doing out here!"

"I can tell you that, Officer Kelton," a voice came from behind them. The two of them jumped like scared pre-schoolers.

Whirling around, they found Lieutenant Harper standing there, trench coat rustling dramatically in the dark, cigarette glowing ominously in his hand.

"Lieutenant!" Kelton said, trying to catch his breath. "Where'd you come from?"

Harper took another drag on his smoke. A little too long of one, as far as Kelton was concerned. Felt like the guy was showing off.

"Where'd I come from? That what you said, Kelton?"

Kelton and Larry exchanged a look.

"Yeah. I just said it. That's how you *know* I said it."

Harper laughed softly, shaking his head.

"That's not the question you should be asking."

Kelton sighed. So this was gonna be one of those.

"What should I be asking, Lieutenant?"

Harper breathed out cigarette smoke like a silvery cloud.

Then promptly started coughing.

Larry and Kelton looked away, waiting for the fit to subside.

"What you should be asking is *not* where I came from. But where I'm *going*. Where *all* of us will be going."

"Uh… not really following you here, Lieutenant," Larry said. "O'course, that may be because of the shoes."

He shook out his right foot as he said that.

"Spirits, officers, that's what I'm talking about. Spirits. That essence of ourselves that lives on after we have shuffled off this mortal coil."

"Right. Hamlet. Act three, scene one," Larry said proudly.

Kelton and Harper stared at him in wonder.

"What? I can't have layers?" Larry asked, embarrassed.

"Spirits? What does that have to do with anything, Lieutenant? What does that have to do with what's been happening here?" Kelton said exasperatedly.

Harper shook his head.

"It's got *everything* to do with it, Officer Kelton! Get your head out of the clouds and down here in the muck with the rest of us! Don't you see? Spirits are mixed up in this whole case! Too many strange things, too many aspects we don't understand! What else could it be but spirits?"

Larry raised his hand meekly.

"Yes, Officer Larry Larry," Harper sighed.

"Just to say, Lieutenant, I mean… isn't that true of anything? We could use that excuse for any situation that the answer or solution isn't readily available for, right? And in that way, we become victims of our own speculations, trapped in a circle of faux rationalizations for actions that we cannot easily explain away. And to me, that's more dangerous than any ghost that ever haunted this plane of existence, if, in fact, any such thing ever has."

Harper was stunned. Kelton, however, nodded in approval.

"Kid said it. *Layers.*"

"That was… amazingly and surprisingly well-said, Officer. And I take your point. But the truth is something is happening here that we don't understand and don't have the capacity to grasp. Not yet anyway."

"Maybe it's just hysterics," Kelton offered.

Harper took another drag off his cigarette.

"Go on, Officer. I'm listening."

"It's like this, Lieutenant. Women. They're prone to it, right? Hysterics? Becoming hysterical? Going off on all kinds of tangents, seeing things that aren't there. You know— communists, Catholics, beatniks, Republicans, all kinds of things! What with all that… all that *plumbing* they got down in there, mysterious systems that we don't really under- stand… I feel that's the source of all this trouble!"

There was a long pause, which, ultimately, made Kelton feel uncomfortable.

"Now we know why you're single, Kelton. We're gonna pretend you didn't say any of that. Next time you wanna make a speech, check with Larry first," Harper declared.

Larry was chuffed to beat the band. Kelton, however, wilted like basil left too long on the windowsill.

"No, gentlemen, it's not any of that. It's spirits. Oh, and the flying saucers."

Kelton and Larry's mouths fell all the way open.

"Saucers!?!" they said in perfect unison.

"Yes indeed. Saucers. Which is the possible source for our mysterious spirits," Harper said. "Just to circle the wagons on that point."

Before either officer could say a word, Harper waved an arm.

"C'mon, let's keep searching this goddamn boneyard. See if we can find anything that'll help us make heads or tails of what's been going on here."

"I swear, I get turned around in here so easily," Larry said. "Plus my shoes apparently constrict my feet in such a way it makes me move in wide right turns."

"What?" Harper asked in confusion.

"Let that one go, Lieutenant," Kelton said.

They hadn't gone more than a few feet when the trio of cops came across a disturbed grave, the headstone knocked down.

"Ah, Christ," Harper said. "Another one. Whoever is paying for these plots should ask for their money back."

"This looks familiar," Kelton said.

"That's 'cause it's a cemetery. It all looks the same," Harper said, bored.

"No, Lieutenant," Larry chimed in. "Kelton's right. There's something familiar about this spot in particular."

Harper raised his arms in frustration.

"Like what? The dirt? The trees? The dark, featureless sky? The drab, gray nothingness of it all? What, exactly, is familiar, with all of this?" Harper said before tripping over the headstone and face-planting into the overturned earth.

"I don't like to kick a man when he's down, but that was kind of funny," Larry said.

Harper pushed himself up and shook the soil off his face.

"Goddamnit," he muttered, bracing himself against the stone, brushing it off as he stood up, not looking at it.

But Kelton did.

"Lieutenant!" he gasped, pointing down at the headstone. "Look!"

Harper looked down, now understanding why this looked familiar to the two officers.

The headstone read—CLAY.

And the inspector was gone.

CHAPTER
SIXTEEN

Colonel Tom Edwards click-clacked his way down the hallowed halls of the Pentagon. The sound reverberated through the marble walkways.

Mostly because Edwards insisted on wearing tap shoes with his dress uniform.

When he was a kid, Edwards hadn't proven to have much aptitude for… well… *anything*… really. He wasn't good at sports. He had a hard time with math. Couldn't diagram a sentence to save his life. Arts and crafts were washouts (signs of these were *very* early on: When he was five, his parents stuck young Tom in a finger-painting class. When they came back to pick him up, they found Tom outside, covered in paint, the doors locked and the lights out, with a note pinned to him saying *'Take him away! Please!'* No further information was forthcoming).

In short, Tom Edwards wasn't good at a damn thing. Until —in utter desperation to get her son out of the house and find something to occupy his time—his mother signed him for tap lessons when he was ten. It was a Hail-Mary-kind-of play.

And to her (and everyone else's) shock—young Tom proved to have not only an aptitude, but a *gift* for tap. That little bastard could tap to beat the band, tap for days. Any routine he was shown, he picked up on it within minutes and could repeat it precisely. He was so good, he dropped out of school to tap full time.

Tapping at dance halls, at recitals, with orchestras, with big bands, on stages all over Pennsylvania (where he grew up), in talent shows, on television (just twice, but still). The future seemed bright for Tom. He was pulling his weight. People loved his act. And he was happy.

Tapping is life, he'd say when people asked him about his newly found passion.

But alas—as if so often the case in this cold world—such joy was not to last.

One night, when Tom was about nineteen, he was following a vaudeville act, a comedy duo. Real physical comedy stuff, slapstick. Pies in the face, tumbles, and the like. The highlight of the act was a "slipping-on-a-banana-peel" bit, wherein one half of the duo would throw the peel on the stage, and the other, not seeing it (wink, wink), steps on it, slips up into the air, completing a full somersault and then landing in the arms of his partner, no worse for wear.

They claimed to have imported the slipperiest banana peels in the Western Hemisphere, from a small, artisanal farm in Ecuador. They ranked a "9" on the Silvan Scale of Slipperiness, according to some reports.

In any event, the gag went off without a hitch: The somersault, the landing, the whole bit.

The audience ROARED with approval at the act, but somehow, in all the hullabaloo following, one peel was left innocuously on stage.

So when Tappin' Tom Edwards came out to do his routine, he didn't know a hazard was there, waiting, like a great white shark below the surface.

There he was, in mid-dance, doing his world-renowned Shim-Sham, when that shark struck. His right foot stepped on the peel and up in the air went Tappin' Tom, only to come down *hard* on the deck, knocking him out in the process.

They say that, even as Tom was being stretchered off the stage, one foot kept tapping, unwilling to give up the ghost.

Since that day, Tom has been unable to tap effectively again. Something about nerve damage to his big toe. But no one knew for sure. Some suspected it was fear, more than anything, that kept Tom off the professional dancing boards.

He joined the military. Proved adept at following orders, served with distinction in Korea and moved up the ranks, becoming a colonel.

It wasn't a bad life, to be sure. But every now and then, like on a stormy night when the rain beats against the window glass, Tom would stare out into the middle distance, hearing that tap of the storm like the taps of his heart, when all there was in the world was dancing.

Now, as a gesture to his past, and to his former passion, whenever he wore his dress uniform, he would slip on his patent leather tap shoes. A bit of individualism in a sea of compliance.

Upon finally reaching his destination, Tom knocked on an office door and waited. Nervous, he did the tiniest bit of a shuffle step. It was all he could manage these days and it helped keep him calm.

A moment later, from within, a gruff voice barked out.

"Get in here, Edwards! On the double-quick!"

Tom swallowed hard and opened the door.

General Roberts sat behind his desk, covered with maps, radar read-outs, and all manner of paperwork. There was also a large candy dish filled with butterscotch candies. The kind that grandmothers give out on Halloween.

Word was Roberts couldn't get enough of the stuff.

"General," Tom said with a salute. "You wanted to see me, sir?"

Without looking up, Roberts grunted. "Sit down, Colonel. Lots to discuss."

Tom looked around.

There wasn't a chair.

So he sat on the floor, cross-legged style.

"All right, Edwards, tell me what the hell happened out there. What was all that goddamn cannon fire? From what I hear, you didn't hit much other than the Washington goddamn Monument! Goddamnit!'

Tom cleared his throat. General Roberts always made him nervous. He did his best to fight it down.

"Apologies, General. I have filed all the appropriate paperwork about repairs to the Monument. But the action was a matter of national security. Flying saucers were attacking us! Beings from another world, sir! UFOs!"

Roberts scoffed. Repeatedly. And he reached out for handful of candies and shoveled them into his mouth, slurping and crunching as he did.

"Ha! Saucers? I don't believe one word of that bunk, Colonel. There's no such thing as flying saucers."

"But, with all respect, General," Tom said, trying to look over the edge of the desk from his vantage point on the floor, "there's plenty of evidence, not the least of which is that dozens and dozens of military personnel saw them! There's pictures in the paper!"

More butterscotches went into Roberts' mouth.

Seriously… how many of those candies could one man eat at one time? Tom tried counting them, but it was no small task.

"Nonsense. Mass hysteria. Faked images!" Roberts slobbered out.

Tom had to stand up, his toes tapping on the tile as he tumbled to his feet.

"General, sir, you weren't there! I was! I saw these things with my own eyes!"

Roberts stood in response, slapping his fist on his desk, causing the candies to dance out of their bowl and skitter across the surface. Roberts scooped them up like ants on the run and shoved them into his mouth.

"Goddamnit! You're begging for a court martial, Colonel!" he said, spewing bits of butterscotch everywhere, including on Tom's face.

"If that's the price for speaking the truth, then I'll take it, General. I know the reality of what I'm saying."

Roberts glowered at Tom, a little drool spilling out of his mouth as it was absolutely stuffed with candy.

Tom tried to imagine the dental bill, but remembered his poor math skills and quickly gave it up. He instead maintained what he hoped was a dignified silence.

Finally, after what seemed like an eternity, Roberts nodded in approval.

"Well done, Colonel. Well done. Holding your ground, maintaining conviction. You can wear those ballet shoes in combat, far as I'm concerned."

"Uh, *tap* shoes, General. Thank you, but I don't—"

Roberts held up his hand, stopping Edwards cold.

"No time for that now, Colonel. We need to discuss a further development regarding these... visitors. Take a seat!"

Tom looked down at the office floor. He didn't want to sit down there again. Besides being cold, it was just... *littered* with bits of butterscotch. All over the place. And he was pretty sure insects were making off with them like bandits.

"General? With all respect, would it be all right if I stood?"

Roberts chuckled.

"Just a like a dancer, eh, Edwards? Better on your feet!"

"Ah... I don't... I mean... maybe..."

Roberts strode over to a small console with what looked like a record player on top.

"Listen to this, Colonel, and tell me how the hell you'd dance to this!"

Roberts dropped the needle on the record (like the kids do) and stood back, arms folded, face in concentration.

For a moment, there was nothing but the usual crackle and hiss of vinyl. Tom didn't understand what he was supposed to be hearing.

And then... there it was!

Voices! Strange, unusual, a language the likes of which Tom had never come across in all his years in the military.

"Good lord, General, what the hell is this?"

"I think you know, Colonel," Roberts said, shoving more candy into his gob.

Listening closely, Tom let the sound wash over him, just like when he was first learning to tap. That was the only way to get the true sense of it.

"Oh my... this is... this is the aliens, isn't it, sir? This changes everything!"

Roberts leaned over and paused the recording, sitting on the edge of his desk.

"Sure is, Colonel. We know those space bastards can talk up a storm! And now we know what their intentions are!"

Tom was as confused as ever.

"What do you mean, General? I can't make sense of whatever it is that they're saying. How can we know their intentions?"

Roberts smiled.

"With the help of this!"

He flicked a switch on a small machine sitting next to the record player. And then sent the recording spinning around the turntable a second time.

The words started again, but this time, after a brief delay... the alien tongue was translated into English!

"Hold the phone, General—are you telling me that we've developed the technology to translate languages in real time?"

"We sure have, Colonel. Best keep it under your hat for now, though. We don't want word of this tech leaking out."

"But... but... imagine what this could do! For people around the world!"

"Like who? Like what?"

Tom scrambled for answers.

"The French!"

"Cheese-eating surrender monkeys."

"The Chinese!"

"Firework-spewing Commie dragons."

"The Soviets!"

"Potato-peel-vodka-drinking sons-of-bitches."

"But General—"

But Roberts shook his head, stopping the recording.

"I'm not having this discussion, Colonel. Firstly, it's above both of our pay grades. Second of all, all that matters right now are these damn aliens. So, let's give a listen to this, and then you tell me what you make of it."

With that, he turned the recording on once again and the eerie voices came through the speakers...

"People of Earth... my name is Eros. Rest assured we mean you no harm. We have come to your world with a message of glorious peace and welcome. You are not alone in the universe. There are civilizations of all kinds, out here, amongst the stars!

There are many, like us, the Klezmers, that look like you, human in appearance. There are others that resemble things out of myth: Demons. Angels. Serpents. Those weird little bugs that roll into balls. All kinds of creatures, finding their homes in the vast cosmos of deep space!

Most of the time, these societies live together in harmony. Plus... you know... the universe is *big*. Really big. Lots of room. So you're not elbowing each other in the ribs. That's pretty key to a happy intergalactic web of peoples. Separate beds make a happy marriage and all that.

But—there has been a wave of concern, shooting through the universe like water from the spray-spout of the whatch-adoolittle. That's the Klezmer version of your whale. Except the blowhole isn't where you think it is. Don't think about it too much.

As we were saying! Concern, rippling out, eventually reaching us. What is that concern, you may ask? Go ahead. Ask. We'll wait.

(At this point in the recording, there were several minutes of silence.)

Thanks for asking. The concern is the creation of your hydrogen bomb. A terrible weapon that can only be used for destruction. If not of yourselves, then likely your neighbors.

Like us.

If humanity continues down this path of weapons development, eventually you will uncover the most dreaded element in all the universe! Solaronite! A substance so powerful that even stars themselves explode when struck by it!

There has long been a universal pact prohibiting the pursuit of solaronite. That and an iron-clad agreement to prevent the sale of whatchadoolittle sperm as an aphrodisiac.

Regardless, as your species is primitive and uncultured, you can't be expected to make such decisions on your own. Thus, the Klezmers have chosen to engage with you, in hopes of preventing galactic armageddon some time in the future.

Allow our ships to land peacefully and without harm. We assure you we have come, not to conquer the earth, but rather to save you from yourselves.

We admit that some of our methods may seem… criminal to you. But that's merely your limited ability to understand the larger stakes that make them appear so.

Rest assured, people of earth! If you do not comply with the demands placed upon you, a fate more terrible than whatchadollittle sputum being spewed upon you will befall your planet! Plans are in motion that… well… just 'plan.'

Just a single plan. We tried others, but they didn't work, so we're just doing the one plan now—but it sounds strange to say 'Plan is in motion' rather than 'Plans are in motion.' Right? There's something off about that. Just falls on the ear in a weird way. Anyway. You get it. *Plans* are in motion to assure the greater safety of the galaxy, whether you like it or not.

This is Eros, of the planet Klezmer, and the people of the same name, signing off."

(This was followed by muffled mumbling and fumbling of someone trying to turn off the recorder. And them something that sounded like, '*Goddamnit!*')

General Roberts switched off the recording.

"Well, Colonel. What do you make of that?"

Tom shook his head. This reminded him of that time he was asked to tap dance out the Star-Spangled Banner to open up a beauty pageant. Just confusing.

"I don't know, General. I've never heard the like of it before. Do we think it's credible?"

"We sure do, Colonel. That's why you're being sent to Hollywood, California. You're to head up our defense there. As well as take over the public relations arm of our film production company."

"Ah, General, with all respect, I'm not qualified to do that."

"We know that, Edwards. The way you handled the defense of Washington proves that to be the case."

"No, sorry, General Roberts, what I meant was—"

"Your flight leaves at oh-six-hundred, Colonel. I suggest you get packed. And bone up on all the latest news regarding labor relations in the cinematographers' union. Dismissed."

Tom stood frozen at first, mouth agape for a moment, but did as ordered.

As he tic-tacked his way down the halls, he couldn't help but wonder:

Was now the time for him to finally become a star?

He did a couple of time steps as he headed out.

CHAPTER
SEVENTEEN

The Ruler was none too pleased.

For one thing, he finally found out what his subordinates meant when they called him 'The Ruler.'

For another thing, this whole Earth operation was a damn mess.

He had summoned Eros and Tanna back to the station, along with their escort flight of two ships. The Ruler had also demanded they bring the reanimated dead back with them for his personal inspection.

Their ship docked, and they immediately reported to The Ruler.

"Ruler," Eros said, making the customary salute.

The Ruler's eyes narrowed slightly as he clocked Tanna making the tiniest, most infinitesimal smirk.

Ohhh, I'll get them for this, he thought to himself, but that would have to wait. There were larger matters demanding his attention.

"Eros," he said coldly. "Report."

Eros cleared his throat. Rather dramatically. And for an *excessively* long period of time.

Seriously, it was like five minutes or something.

"Apologies, Ruler. I must have caught viral infection on that inferior mudball of a planet,"

Eros said finally. "And that concludes my report."

He turned on his heels to go, fingers crossed.

"Hold, Eros," The Ruler said. "That report seems not fully fleshed out. So why not turn around, face me and tell me WHY THIS WHOLE THING IS A DISASTER??"

The whole room shuddered in reaction.

… And it wasn't just the room that was shuddering…

Tanna had never heard The Ruler raise his voice before. She had to admit, it was doing something for her. She licked her lips, thinking about mass ordering some new straight-edges. For her office, of course.

"Yes, Ruler," Eros finally managed to get out, cowering slightly in the process. "I will admit… things have not gone *quite* according to plan, but—"

"Not *QUITE*?!?" The raging Ruler roared rapaciously. "You were told to keep it quiet. Our ships are on the front page of every news outlet on the Earth! You were engaged in combat with American military forces! And why are you obsessed with that one cemetery, for Klezmer's sake?"

Eros felt himself go flushed. He wasn't great at confrontation. That was true of his entire life. But it had only gotten worse since joining the space command forces. Once, he had been reprimanded by his commander for not making his bunk properly.

He hid in the bathroom stall for three days.

If only there was a bathroom nearby now, Eros thought desperately.

"Ruler, allow me to explain," he began, but The Ruler slammed his fist down on his desk console.

Tanna quickly ordered some new *personal* implements on her mobile device, her breath getting shorter.

"No explanations can explain this!"

Eros looked at him quizzically.

"Well. Technically speaking, that's what explanations *do*," he said foolishly.

The Ruler hauled off and slapped him across the face. And Tanna had to excuse herself.

"Pardon me… I need to… take care of something," she muttered and rushed out of the room, legs squirming the whole time.

"I'm relieving you of command of the two additional ships you had been given, Eros," The Ruler said, stalking back behind his desk and sitting down.

"But—but, Sir—!"

"Not another word, Eros, or I'll suspend this entire operation! You've been mucking about, from one mistake to another, without any clear goals or, indeed, any tangible effects on the human populace!"

Eros was humbled. He knew this was true, but he was also convinced that this was the only way to prevent the future creation of solaronite, which could be the death of every living being in the galaxy.

"I hear you, Ruler, and your concerns are well-founded, but I firmly believe that this is the right course that we are on!"

The Ruler sighed with great flair, sitting down (gingerly as always) into his chair.

"Fine, Eros, fine. I'll give you one last chance to correct these errors and right the ship. Otherwise, I'm yanking you fully from command. Is that understood?"

Eros bowed as deeply as he could. Which was pretty deep. He'd been stretching.

Tanna appeared back in the doorway, face glowing.

"Apologies, all. I… had to… uh… press a button. But I did so. Successfully. Very successfully. More than once. So. Yeah. Everything's good now."

Eros and The Ruler stared at her blankly for a moment as she smiled dreamily.

"Eros, let me see this reanimated corpse weapons you've

created," The Ruler said, turning his attention back to the matter at hand.

"At once, Ruler," Eros said and nodded curtly to Tanna. She tossed her hair seductively to one side as she swept out of the room.

A moment later she returned, electrode gun at the ready, with the Ghoul Man & Woman and the undead Inspector Clay. The three creatures stood at attention, waiting to be commanded.

The Ruler leapt to his feet, a spring in his step, at the sight of the beasts.

"Okay, this is something. This could be a thing. Show me what they can do," he said animatedly.

"As you command, dear Ruler," Eros said, looking to Tanna, who nodded.

Activating the gun, she aimed it at Clay, who lurched forward clumsily, like a car kept in park too long.

With blank, black eyes and an open, drooling mouth (Eros made note of that. Drooling was a curious side effect of the reanimation process. It didn't serve any purpose, as these things didn't eat and had no need for saliva. Huh), Clay lumbered forward, powerful arms rising, bear-like hands grasping out.

"Excellent," The Ruler said, clapping. "Make it do something, Tanna. Make it do something *bad*."

"Okay," she said, giggling, and directed Clay towards Eros.

"Uh… hold up, now," Eros said, alarmed. "Let's not get—GACK!"

Clay wrapped his meathook hands around Eros' throat, throttling him.

"Puh—please—s-s-sstoppp," he sputtered out, even as The Ruler's joy grew exponentially.

"Oh, this is *fabulous*. Make him do more!"

Tanna obliged.

Clay picked Eros up by the throat, whacking him up and down like a rubber ball.

(Now—no need for concern. Klezmers have remarkable constitutions, with ligaments that stretch like elastic, so really, Eros was fine. Well, not "fine"-fine, but he'd be alright.

Probably.)

Eros' face was turning purple. And while that *was* a flattering color on him, The Ruler decided enough was enough.

Plus, he was already getting bored.

Which was a pretty common state for him actually, so nobody needed to be too surprised. Apart from Eros, that is. He was pretty surprised by the whole situation, really.

"Release him, Tanna," he said off-handedly.

With a wisp of disappointment on her face, Tanna did as ordered. Clay released Eros, who dropped like a sack of old potatoes.

...*Or* a sack of rucklethacks.

'Rucklethacks' were a Klezmer vegetable, dark yellow in color, wrinkled like fingers in a pool, that only grew on the north side of the mountains of the Slicketty Crank Range.

According to legend, rucklethacks had the nutrients necessary to... ah... *embolden*... the male mating drive. However, it was perilous to harvest these weird little things. Many a "lacking-in-virility" Klezmer fella had fallen to his death along those sheer cliffs.

It had been suggested, more than once, that rucklethacks did *not*, in fact, possess such enhancements, but rather it was a ploy by Klezmer women to—one—Keep the boys away and two—Weed out the stupid and inferior for the greater good of the genetic pool.

Either way, Eros hit the deck *hard*.

"Impressive," said The Ruler admiringly. "And it leads me to build in a modification of the plan we are currently enacting."

"Modification?" Eros spat out as he climbed to his feet, trying to recover some dignity.

"Yes, indeed," The Ruler said. "This brute has inspired me. You are to keep him in reserve as long as possible. Use this cloaked one as a distraction, keeping the humans confused and afraid, even if it means his capture."

"But, Ruler—"

"Silence, Eros! My will is not to be questioned, least of all by *you*!"

Tanna felt herself getting warm all over again.

"Then, you will find sufficient numbers of human dead like this... this hulking creature! We will raise an ARMY of such monsters! When they are assembled fully, we will march them on all of Earth's capitals, *forcing* humanity to come to heel!"

He laughed then, throwing his head back.

It sounded slightly like a donkey.

In heat.

Being branded.

And just as quickly as it came on, it stopped.

Snapping his head forward, he looked at them.

"You are dismissed, Eros. See about this plan. Make it work. Or face the consequences."

"Yes, Ruler, of course."

He turned to go, Tanna following, but before they were out the door—

"Tanna. A moment."

She turned back, cheeks rosy as apples and breath coming quickly.

"I'd like to discuss that... *button*, with you, if I may. Eros, you may go."

Eros opened his mouth to respond but thought better of it.

He left the room, door sliding closed behind him, wondering what the hell kind of button was so important.

...Which pretty much summed him up in a nutshell.

CHAPTER
EIGHTEEN

Tom Edwards sighed heavily. This wasn't what he signed up for. Nor was it what he expected when he was given these orders to report to "Hollywood."

To begin with—Burbank wasn't Hollywood. Not by a long shot. Oh, sure, it was *adjacent* to Hollywood, but it wasn't the Silver City, no way.

Okay, so maybe they filmed some *television* in Burbank. And Tom was certain those folks worked hard, but as far as artistic quality and expression?

Nah, no way.

Movies were what mattered! Movies captured people's imaginations, told them stories they'd never seen before, created worlds beyond conception.

On the flight out to the West Coast from Washington, Tom couldn't help but daydream. About the movies. The stories that could be told about the frustrated tap dancer, who decided that serving his country was the better pursuit.

And defend it he did! From alien invaders from another world, no less! After such heroics, what was the reward for such a servant of the people? Why, fulfilling the destiny he was promised! By becoming America's favorite tap-dancing star, full of light and glory—complete with awards, accolades, several ill-advised affairs with bombshells and femme fatales, ending it all with a run as an elder statesman of show business, complete with a star on the Hollywood Walk of Fame and endless eulogies upon his leaving this plane of existence.

Yeah. None of that was happening in goddamn *Burbank*.

Even that *name*.

Burbank.

It inspired nothing, except maybe the need for an antacid.

So Tom was disappointed, to put it mildly.

Even more so when, upon landing, he was whisked off from the airport, along a winding road that led to a lone house sitting by a cemetery, just off the airport property. When he'd gotten out of the car, Tom looked at the house in wonder. Who in the hell would choose to live all the way out here, surrounded by rotting corpses, mourning relatives and the *constant* sound of planes coming and going?

As he walked up the drive to the front door, he tried a little shuffle-step to pick up his spirits, but the ground was gravel, as opposed to concrete or masonry.

So it sounded like trash.

"This blows," he muttered to himself, knocking on the door.

After a moment, the door swung open, to reveal a creature in an iron mask, thick gloves, eyes aglow, with a burning flame in its hand!

"Jesus Christ, they're moving in!" Tom exclaimed, stumbling backwards and reaching for his sidearm.

The gun was in one of those belt holsters that has the little button. And he couldn't snap that damn thing open.

"Stay—stay back, Beast From Beyond!" Tom sputtered, desperately trying to get to his weapon.

"Hold on, Colonel," a muffled voice said from behind the iron mask.

The flame shut off, and Tom realized it was a welder's torch. And the mask to match.

The creature flipped the mask up and there, smiling, was Paula Trent.

"Sorry to have startled you, Colonel," Paula said. "I've been working on a new sculpture made from found materials. No commission for this one yet, it's just how I unwind after a stressful time. You know how we women can be!"

She reached out a hand and Tom, possibly more afraid and more turned on than he'd ever been in his life, took it carefully.

"We've been expecting you. My husband, Jeff, is waiting for you right inside. He would've gotten the door himself, as he's only three feet away and I was out in the garage, but really, what's a wife for if not to answer the door?"

Tom opened his mouth to reply, but was nervous the words 'I love you' and 'Please be my queen for all time and eternity' would come out.

So he just shut it instead and stepped inside the Trent home.

Jeff Trent was reading the paper, smoking a pipe.

Tom clocked the headline. It read:

SAUCERS?????????

???????????????????

??????????????????

It seemed like an excessive use of the question mark, but Tom wasn't an editor.

"Captain Trent," Tom said, offering a hand.

Jeff stood, putting the paper to the side. (Tom could see the question marks extended past the fold.)

"Colonel. Please call me Jeff. I'm only 'Captain' up in the air. And in the bedroom, of course."

"Oh, Jeff. Silly," Paula said, swatting him with a gloved hand.

How Tom would have loved to be on the receiving end of that swat.

"Jeff. Please call me Tom. As I'm sure you know, the military brass asked me to come out here to talk with you about what you've seen and experienced. Would you be willing to have that conversation with me?"

"Of course, Tom, but only on one condition," Jeff countered.

"If it's sleeping with your wife, consider it done, Jeff."

Jeff stared at him.

Tom froze.

Did he say that out loud?

"Did I say that out loud?"

"Sure did, Tom. And I'll tell you what... we can talk about it. But let's let her finish with her little project first. God knows you don't want that flame turned on you!"

He chuckled and Tom joined in, even though, honestly, he wasn't so sure he'd mind the torch.

"Just a joke, Jeff. An odd little icebreaker we learn over at the Pentagon, that's all. Forgive the familiarity. What was your question?" Tom said, attempting to recover.

"The brass. ...Is it?"

The question hung in the air.

"Is it... what, Jeff? I'm not following."

"*Is* it brass? I've always wondered about that. You hear that phrase all the time. 'The Brass." And I've never really understood it. Are the leaders of the military men of brass? Like Doc Bronze, but brass? Is that what happens upon promotion? You get dipped in brass? Like how parents used to dip baby shoes? Remember that? But anyway, are all the top commanders, you know, clanking around in the Pentagon? 'Cause they're covered in brass?"

Jeff paused, eyes alight, full of wonder and curiosity.

Tom thought about what to do here.

Play along, he decided. *Best not to upset him.*

"You bet they are, Jeff. Now, keep that quiet. That's something we don't want the civilian population to know. You understand."

"I KNEW IT!" Jeff shouted, raising his arms triumphantly. "But no fears, Colonel. I'm going to keep it quiet. *For now.*" He laughed then. And Tom wanted to punch him.

"Good job, Jeff," is what he said instead. "Now, about your encounters with the alien spacecraft—"

"I'm not sure what else I can add to the official reports, Tom. I laid it out pretty much as it happened. They do seem kind of obsessed with our little stretch of land here and I can't say that I exactly understand why."

Tom scoffed.

"Me neither."

Jeff stiffened at that.

"What do you mean by that?"

"No, nothing, nothing," Tom said, scrambling.

"You have a problem with our neighborhood?" Jeff asked demandingly.

"Not at all, not at all," Tom replied, holding up his hands in a peaceful way. "No, I just mean, you know… the cemetery and all."

"But it's quiet!"

"Yeah. But the planes? Not actually quiet, right? Actually pretty noisy."

Jeff didn't know what to say.

"Sure, yeah, but… it's close to work!"

"Right, I hear that, but does that convenience really make that much of a difference? For one thing, you're essentially on call, at all times, because they know you're here. So whenever someone bails on a shift, you're on, Captain. No real time off, there."

"He's got a point, Jeff," Paula said, popping her head into the room, wearing nothing but her soot-stained overalls.

It's intentional, Tom thought. *She's doing this deliberately. Little vixen.*

"But… but… the *cost,*" Jeff stammered out.

Paula sauntered in, looking like ten miles of bad road that Tom would give anything to pave.

"I checked the books, hon. You know how you are with numbers and all. We're actually *losing* money on this dump, because somehow, the value is decreasing every day. Probably because of all the murders nearby. And how I was chased out of the house by that strange creature, only to be rescued by Farmer Calder, whom you gave a one dollar tip and then sent him on his way, which caused *him* to tell everyone that we've got a *mold* problem. The house is now worth three times *less* than when we bought it."

Tom had become so worked up during that little monologue, had to readjust himself, even as Jeff sat back down, stunned.

"Well. I hadn't considered all that," he said, defeatedly.

"Of course not, babe. You're far too busy to be worrying about such things. That's a wife's job, after all," Paula said with a bright smile and headed back out.

Gotta have that woman, Tom thought.

"Gotta have that woman!"

He closed his eyes.

"Christ, did I do it again?"

"Sure did, Tom, but there's no time for that now. You were talking about the saucers?"

"That's right, Jeff. Did you happen to notice anything about the wind pressure prior to the saucers arriving? We have a theory that's something which could be used to detect them in a timely fashion."

"It's funny you say that, Colonel. My co-pilot Danny—you can meet him later. He's tied up in a leather mask in the back bedroom, waiting for his punishment period to end—did some calculating on that very thing. And we came to the same conclusion!"

Tom nodded. He had suspected as much.

"This is great news, Jeff. Thanks for sharing. I've got to report it back to—"

"—The brass?" Jeff said eagerly.

Tom rolled his eyes, just slightly.

"You bet, buddy. Hang tight. I'm going to want to talk to you some more."

Tom excused himself and headed back to his car. There was a military radio built in so he could communicate with the Pentagon and tell them what's what.

Plus… he wanted to see if he could find any of that used soot from Paula and rub it all over himself.

CHAPTER
NINETEEN

THE LONE SAUCER that was now afforded to Eros to command descended silently into the cemetery.

Again.

It was truly *was* a wonder that no cemetery employees, nor any of the *other* pilots, crew, and staff at the nearby Burbank airport, nor any of the seemingly *dozens* of police officers currently searching the grounds, nor any mourners or visitors to the graveyard managed to catch a single glimpse of the spacecraft as it repeatedly landed in their collective backyard.

But there *was* an unknown and singular factor that the Klezmers, alone amongst all the intelligent species in the universe, were in possession.

Luck.

Now, conventional wisdom has it that luck—A) doesn't really exist and—B) is really just happenstance. Coincidence.

Chance, in other words.

But the Klezmer scientific community spent a considerable amount of time and resources researching this phenomenon known on Earth as "luck", but on planet Klezmer, it was known as "frigglefrack."

Parenthetically, the word came from the experience of one

Dr. Atumal Sloran, considered a great mind in the Klezmer community.

Dr. Sloran was hiking along the trails of the dreaded Mt. Hoffensnuffer, the largest, active volcano on Klezmer. Geologists, meteorologists and tour guides had issued warnings about the volcano on this particular spring day, saying it was unstable and likely to blow at any second, spewing lava, ash, and noxious gas into the air.

Dr. Sloran (often accused of being full of noxious gas himself) had ignored such warnings. Although his area of expertise was genetics, and he couldn't tell you if it was raining after looking at the sky, Sloran scoffed at the deterrence because he wanted to go for a walk and look down into the valley beneath Mt. Hoffensnuffer.

He could be a bit of a prig, that Dr. Sloran.

So, up he went, along the slopes of the volcano. Sure enough, not ten minutes into his hike, BOOM goes the mountain.

A veritable *geyser* of smoke and debris shot in the atmosphere, obscuring visibility for miles and threatening the population down below in the valley with utter destruction.

And yet...

Sloran had been walking with his trusty carbon-diamond walking stick; firm, sturdy, unbreakable. Ridiculously expensive and impossibly vain. When the eruption occurred, he was flung backwards at a terrific speed, flailing back against another cliff side.

His walking stick, which he had gripped for dear life, struck the cliff face in such a specific spot that it triggered a tremendous rock slide, sending ancient stone tumbling down the mountain.

It managed to gather in almost a dam-like fashion, and the lava that burst forth from the top of the volcano was steered by this new rock formation and spilled harmlessly into another crevasse, feeding it back into itself. It created a loop, with the lava spilling out and flowing back in.

In the end, it became a tourist and research attraction, known as "Sloran's Slurry." Klezmers the world over would come to marvel at the inner workings of their planet through this unique vantage point.

As for Sloran himself, he became so *convinced* that what he had managed was more than just luck, he dedicated the entirety of his career to the study of it. He searched for a way to prove that luck could be engineered and believed it could be done through the manipulation of the genetic code.

But how did he reach this conclusion?

To begin with, he did extensive studies on all Klezmers who had experienced greater luck than average: Surviving impossible accidents, winning lotteries at a prodigious rate, being selected for various fellowships and prizes, and so on.

Next, he did genetic research on those individuals to determine whether there was a common factor in their genes that could account for such good fortune.

Finally, he took that research and developed a serum, not unlike an inoculation, given right after birth, that imparted all Klezmers with this seemingly random bit of luck.

It was known as *Frigglefrack* because that's what Sloran onomatopoetically said was the noise he heard when the volcano exploded.

Sounds great, right?

Yeah. Not so much.

Because if *everyone* is lucky, then there can't be a winner.

Lotteries started pulling out multiple entries at the same time. Accidents became MORE fatal because either EVERYONE lived or EVERYONE died. Professional sports leagues dried up because a winner could never be determined. Everything ended in a tie.

So it wasn't long before this serum garnered a nickname of its own: Sloran's Folly. Klezmers got *sick* of their luck. Actually, it was kind of a pain in the ass. If everything goes right all the time, then what does anyone have left to strive for?

Philosophers, politicians, and educators debated it. Entire

schools of thought were dedicated to this question. It appeared on ballots and referendums.

Finally, it was decided that not everyone needs such luck. That good fortune was better made than given.

Frigglefrack, and Dr. Sloan, fell into the dustbins of Klezmer history.

Except in one specific instance:

Every pilot in the Klezmer Space Armada, after reaching the highest level of rank and proficiency, was given the option of taking Frigglefrack. It seemed reasonable that military and special forces should be afforded the opportunity for greater luck.

And Eros had been one of those to take the serum.

Hence his ability to land his craft repeatedly in the same place on a foreign planet without anyone noticing at all.

Thus ends the parenthetical.

The ship landed safely without incident. And soon afterwards, a hatch slid open from its side. From within emerged the Ghoul Man, cape covering his face. He moved nimbly, considering how dead he was.

And how old.

And how impractical his clothing was.

Regardless, off he went into the depths of the cemetery, following some terrible purpose not his own.

Kelton was bored stiff. This detail had to be one of the worst in his long history of bad details. And he'd had more than his share since joining the force.

First, there was the one wherein he had to guard the elephants coming to town as part of the circus. There had been a rumor that an international poaching ring were planning on stealing them for their tusks and the ivory market.

Now, Kelton firmly believed that poaching was every kind of wrong. He was an animal guy all the way through. But still... how the hell do you steal an elephant? Let alone MULTIPLE elephants? That seemed pretty unlikely to him.

But whatever. Orders were orders.

What he didn't expect, however, was the sheer volume of stench and the sheer volume of... *waste*, let us say. It was—to put it mildly— overwhelming. Some would have called it a "shit detail' in a poor attempt at humor.

Well. They had no idea.

Then there was the detail wherein he had to protect a group of mimes.

Yup. Mimes.

Apparently, there had been a bank robbery and a mime troupe, in town for a performance, had somehow managed to be witnesses to the whole thing. They refused to take off their white pancake makeup and, also... *refused to speak*. Wouldn't break the "mime code," whatever the hell that was.

Kelton got stuck making sure they were safe and "unmolested" as the order stated. That's not a word Kelton would've used, but he wasn't the boss.

Listen–the mimes were a pain in the ass. First off, all they did was seemingly complain that they were either—A) stuck in a box or—B) victims of an unusually strong breeze. Secondly, they all smoked. All the time. It was like L.A. smog in the room where they all were staying. The weird bit was that Kelton never saw any actual cigarettes. Just them *pretending* to have cigarettes, but somehow still blowing out actual smoke. He was baffled. And he stank like a tobacco farm on fire for days afterwards.

Rough times.

But even those two details weren't as boring as this one was.

Nothing happening. Nobody around except for other cops. Kelton wasn't even sure what they were looking for. Plus, there was a weird vibe about the whole thing. Mysterious comings and goings, bodies disappearing. Who knew what the hell was going on out here?

It wasn't what Kelton had signed up for, that's for damn sure. He joined the force to make a difference for people... and to get out of the five thousand dollars' worth of parking tickets he had accrued over the years.

As Kelton waited, for *anything*, to happen, he began to smell something. Something wrong. (After the elephants and smoking mimes, Kelton's olfactory senses were *sharp*.)

Whatever it was smelled like old socks and molding fruit. And it was getting *stronger*.

"Hey," Kelton called out to his fellow officers, all of whom were just kind of milling about, pretending to be looking for clues, but actually wondering what the hell they were doing. "Anyone else smell that?" There was a general chorus that ranged from "Nah," "What?" or, "Shut up, Kelton!"

But there *was* a smell. Kelton was positive about that. And the something making that smell was getting closer.

"Guys," Kelton said worriedly, "I'm not trying to be a jerk, but something smells *bad* and whatever the hell it is, it's *here*."

Officer Larry, always quick to be on Keton's side (mostly because Kelton called him "Larry" and not "Larry"), jumped on board.

"Kelton's right. I smell it too."

One of the other uniformed cops on site, named Rock Brockington, scoffed out loud.

"Why don't you just shove it, Larry? Right up where Kelton's sun don't shine."

He laughed, sort of like a sick turkey.

Thing was, Brockington had bad blood with Kelton. Mostly because after he had been divorced, Rock's ex-wife, Stockard, had briefly shacked up with Kelton. Rock and Stock, as they had been known, were forever fighting and it was a surprise to no one when they ended their tumultuous two-month marriage.

Kelton swooping in and snapping up Stock, however, was

pretty much unexpected. Especially given how Kelton smelled like elephant-dung cigarettes most of the time.

That relationship hadn't lasted long. Stock had met a man named Brock. Brock Lockerby. They had moved together to Mock, Washington.

As an interesting sidebar, Mock was classified as an "extinct town," a former logging hub in the Pacific Northwest that had long since been abandoned. Brock was confident that he would be able to reignite that industry all by himself. However, he had no working knowledge of logging nor any equipment of any kind that would have served him in that endeavor.

Stock admired his pluck and resolved to follow Brock wherever he went, including Mock, for good or for ill.

Rock never saw his ex-wife again (in fact, no one ever saw her again, but that's a tale for another time), but he sure held onto his grudge with Kelton. Any opportunity to make him look small was one he would take, ten out of ten times.

"After all," Rock said sneeringly, "Kelton's a fan of stealing another man's sunshine."

Kelton sighed. He'd been putting up with this for years now.

"That don't make no sense, Rock," Kelton said wearily. "Do you even know how to properly insult someone? I mean —you really want to hurt a guy, you take his girl, am I right?" There was a bunch of "Oooooooohs" from all the gathered officers. Everyone knew the story of Rock and Stock and Brock and Mock. And everyone was *always* ready for some drama.

Rock's face had turned bright red.

"You know what, Kelton—" but before he could finish that sentence, the smell Kelton had warned everyone about suddenly became overwhelming. Every cop gathered gagged on it.

"Jesus," Larry cried out, "what *is* that stench?"

Before Rock could say something clever (or at least obvious), he felt a cold hand grasp him on the shoulder.

Whirling around, there was the Ghoul Man, face pale, cape black, and teeth rotting.

Here was the source of that odor; here was the face of the undead!

Now—police were generally trained to have good reaction time. Indeed, an argument could be made that *reaction* is the primary function of their role in society at large. Some would say that perhaps the police were trained to be *too* reactive, but that's not an issue to be addressed here.

Regardless of that, in this moment, faced with something incredible, the threat of an undead creature, controlled by beings from beyond the stars… the cops did… *nothing.*

They didn't react at all. Like… not even a little bit.

Rock stumbled away from the grasp of the Ghoul Man, starting wide-eyed and open-mouthed, but didn't draw his weapon. Nor did anyone else.

"Would ya look at that?" Kelton mumbled to himself, but that was the extent of his response.

Following an ancient herd mentality, the cops all slowly backed up together from the Ghoul Man, forming a little group, huddled together in the face of unnatural evil.

Or something like that.

Kelton looked around at all the terrified faces and shook his head.

"Hey! What are we *doing*?" he called out. "We're the *Burbank* police! We're not afraid of nothin'!"

He pulled out his gun and fired.

Following his lead, every other cop there, including Rock Brockington, pulled out their service revolvers and pulled the trigger, all aiming at the Ghoul Man, eerily silent, terribly smelly, and grimly advancing upon them.

The bullets, however, seemingly had no effect on the approaching monster. The Ghoul Man never wavered, stumbled, fell back… he just kept coming closer, at an agonizingly slow pace.

"Christ, Kelton," Larry said, "what are we gonna do?"

Kelton didn't answer. For one thing, he didn't know. For another thing, he couldn't believe he was going to die stuck next to Rock. He spared a thought to remember Stock. They had a good time together, brief though it was. Kelton wished her well and hoped she would remember him, somewhere in the woods around Mock.

He closed his eyes, assuming that doom was about to befall him and he didn't want to see it coming.

And he waited.

But nothing happened.

Kelton felt someone nudge him.

"Kelton," a whispered voice said. It was Larry. "Take a look!"

Carefully, Kelton opened his eyes, to see all his fellow officers looking in wonder straight ahead.

There was a humming sound, surrounding them all. The Ghoul Man was frozen in place, standing stock still. The only movement was the creature's eyes, which grew wider and wider.

The beast began to shudder and there was a flash of bright blue light and then—

—There was nothing but bones! The Ghoul Man was now just a skeleton!

It stood upright for just a second, as if it had forgotten it no longer had muscles or mind. Then it collapsed in a heap onto the ground, tucked within the folds of the black cape, still tied around its neck.

Larry whistled low.

"Don't see that every day," he said.

Kelton breathed a sigh of relief. He had no idea what had happened, but he knew that he, and the rest of the officers, were safe.

At least for the moment. But he knew it wasn't over. Not yet.

He felt someone gripping his hand suddenly and he

jumped like a black cat during the Salem witch trials. He turned to see Rock, tears rolling down his face.

"Jesus, Rock! Scared the hell outta me!"

"Sorry, Kelton," he sobbed. "I just miss her, is all."

Kelton felt a wave of understanding and nodded with sympathy.

"Me too, buddy. Me too."

CHAPTER
TWENTY

Inside the ship, Eros was steaming. Not only emotionally, but also sartorially. He liked his uniform wrinkle-free and he found that the iron they had on board made everything just a bit too stiff for his liking.

He had spent his own salary (as an aside, the Klezmer monetary system was a bit of a puzzle. It was based on the value of cheese. The Klezmers couldn't get enough of it. Milk-producing animals, called the *tharflu*, were treated like royalty because of the quality of the milk. It was said that Klezmer cheese was known throughout the galaxy as being so good that it would curl the toes of any species, including those *without* toes. So, back at home, the Klezmer people hoarded cheese, aging it, drying it, whatever they could. Legend had it that one brave soul made an ocean-going ship out of hardened cheese. But when he set off to circumnavigate Klezmer, he was never seen again. It was presumed that native aquatic species simply ate through the hull until it sank. Others said he found a remote island, living out the rest of his days slowly consuming his own vessel. The truth was never uncovered. But that aside, the Klezmers used cheese as their currency as well. You'd walk into a shop, searching for... a hat, let us say. You'd hand over the weight equivalent in cheese, and you'd receive the item you'd purchased. Now… the *downside* of this economic system was nearly every Klezmer was constantly constipated. The cheese, despite its deliciousness, was apparently hard to digest. Also, the tharflu only produced milk one month out of the year. If dairy farmers weren't able to harvest enough, the economy would collapse. But most people didn't care. The cheese was *worth* it.) on a steam machine.

He kept that machine in his quarters, secreted away from the rest of the ship. Eros knew that if Tanna got her hands on it, he'd never see it again. So he did all his steaming in private.

Just felt better that way.

But along with this wardrobe care, Eros was pretty upset about the dressing-down he received from The Ruler. To have his skill questioned! His leadership challenged! His plan undercut!

…Also, something *for sure* was happening between The Ruler and Tanna, and Eros had to be honest, he just wasn't sure how he felt about that.

But he knew this: steaming his uniform made him feel better. It took his mind off of things. There was something immensely satisfying about seeing the wrinkles just fall away, disappearing into the smooth fabric.

It should be noted, Eros was also nude while doing these tasks.

As much as Eros loved steaming, he was sensitive to the heat. So he always stripped down to the barest level. He figured that sweating it out was also good for his skin.

Gotta keep the pores healthy, after all.

He was lost in thought and a veil of steam when there was a sudden knock at the cabin door, startling him.

Eros dropped the steamer, bouncing off his feet and scorching him in places that were better left unsaid.

"AHHHH!" he cried out in pain and surprise, scrambling to pick the instrument up off the floor while protecting his bare bits.

The pounding on his door came again and a muffled voice called through:

"Eros! Eros, are you all right?"

It was Tanna, of course. There wasn't any other crew.

Before he could answer, she overrode the door's electronic command and rushed into his cabin, where Eros stood, in all his naked glory.

('Glory' may be a bit of an overreach, but—)

"Eros," Tanna said breathlessly, "what happened? Are you injured—"

She stopped as she got herself a good gander of what all was happening in this room at this moment.

Tanna had never thought much of Eros, truth be told. He was a stickler for the rules, kind of a boor and a bore, and generally wasn't much fun as a commanding officer.

But... well, to be frank... she had no idea he was packing like *this*.

Plus, Tanna had been worked up since the meeting with The Ruler and was hungry for more.

She wasn't sure that Eros would be the right fit (both emotionally and, now, physically. *Damn.*), but it would be fun to think about.

"Well. I see you're... just fine," she said with a wicked smirk.

Eros quickly snatched the steamer from the floor of his cabin and turned it on high, the steam billowing out and forming a cloud cover that would have to do for now.

"Tanna," he said, trying to sound dignified and failing miserably. "Do you have something to report?"

"Only that we've landed undetected. These humans are pretty dumb, Eros. Are we sure they're potentially the threat to the galaxy as you say they are?"

Eros grimaced. The steam was really getting *hooooooooooot.*

"Yes," he squeaked out. "There's no question. But maybe now isn't the time to discuss it at greater length, Tanna."

"Oh, I think we've got all the greater length we need," she purred with a grin.

"Tanna," Eros with a touch of exasperation and a *hint* of pride, "clearly I'm in the middle of something here. Is there something else you want?"

She lightly licked her lips.

"There's plenty I want, but for now, I'll settle for uncloaking the ship."

"What? Why?"

"Part one of the plan has been executed. The first undead has been reduced to his skeletal structure, cluing the humans in that something more profound than they can imagine what is happening. The next step is to bring them *here*. To see who we are and what we are capable of. In order to do that, we *must* uncloak. Let *them* find *us*. Then we'll show them the folly of defying our will!"

Eros considered this. Tanna had sussed it out, and he couldn't see a reason not to follow through with this plan.

He also had dropped the steamer while he was lost in thought and the resounding '*clang*' brought him to his senses.

"All right, Tanna. Point made. Uncloak the ship and see what we can do about luring the humans right to us. It's time to make our presence known!"

Tanna's eyes flickered down for a moment.

"Oh, I'd say our presence is *well*-known at this point, Commander Eros. The most well-known it's ever been, perhaps."

Eros rolled his eyes.

"All right, that's enough. Now get out of here so I can get dressed, for Klezmer's sake."

"Don't rush on my account," Tanna replied and sauntered out of the room, with an extra swish of her hips that Eros had never quite noticed before.

But there were things to attend to, and time couldn't be

wasted any further. He quickly slipped on his uniform, finding it a touch tighter in certain areas than it had been earlier.

CHAPTER
TWENTY-ONE

Colonel Edwards' car arrived at the cemetery entrance and slowly pulled in.

Upon parking, the doors opened, and out came Tom, Jeff, and Paula Trent, four members of the military police, six non-commissioned officers, three Army doctors, nine Green Berets, one staff psychologist, fourteen members of the National Guard, three members of the Army Corps Of Engineers, eight staff from the Army Science Research Center, seven military chaplains (representing different faiths), two hitchhikers they picked up along the way, and five Golden Rings (That was the name for an elite parachute squad).

There was a shocking amount of room in that car, and Tom hadn't been given the budget to approve multiple vehicles. So efficiency was the order of the day.

As the rest of the team shuffled about to their various posts and assignments, Tom pulled Jeff and Paula aside for a moment.

"Mrs. Trent, are you sure you want to be here for this?" he asked carefully.

Paula nodded vigorously.

"You bet I am, Colonel. I know I only made the rank of Sergeant-Major while I was in the service, but I'd still prefer to be here than at home. God knows what kind of trouble I'd be getting myself into if I were alone. As a woman, I just can't be trusted. Besides, I know it makes Jeff feel better. Doesn't it, honey?"

Jeff shook his head.

"Darling, I really need you to be more respectful. The Colonel and I are speaking."

"Right you are, honey. My mistake. Let me see if I can fix that carburetor in the Colonel's car. It seems to be on the fritz."

Paula waltzed over and popped the hood up, while Jeff smiled indulgently, nodding.

"Sorry about that, Colonel," he said with a chuckle. "You know how women can be."

"Actually, she seems pretty capable as far as I can—"

Jeff held up a hand, stopping him mid-thought.

"Just lay out the plan for me here, Colonel. How are we going to stop these space bastards, once and for all?"

"That's something I'd like to know as well," a masculine voice said from behind them, causing Jeff to jump and scramble behind Paula like a three-year-old.

Paula reacted, quickly brandishing a wrench as a weapon.

"Hold on to my skirts, dear," she said. "You shouldn't be expected to handle something like this. It's a female matter."

"Won't be necessary, Mrs. Trent," the voice called from the shadows. And, there, stepping into the light, was Lieutenant Harper, with Kelton and Larry right on his heels.

"I'm sorry, I'm not sure we've met," Tom said, extending his hand.

"Name's Harper, Colonel. Lieutenant, Burbank Police. My inspector was *killed* out here and then *buried* out here and then his resurrected corpse *escaped* and was left wandering around… out here. These men—" he said, sticking a thumb towards the other two, "—also encountered a reanimated corpse of the recent dead. An old man. Who had a thing for Gilded Age drama in his wardrobe choices."

"What?" Jeff asked, his eyes blinking blankly.

"Man liked a cape or cowl, I'm guessing. That about it, Lieutenant?" Tom asked.

Harper nodded solemnly.

"Yessir, Colonel. But I have to say, even that's not the strangest thing going on here."

"If this is about the peanut-butter brittle and group hair waxing, I can explain all of that," Jeff offered sheepishly, but Paula put a reassuring hand on his arm.

"I know I couldn't possibly be expected to understand, love, but I don't think the events of your bachelor party are what's under discussion," she said calmly.

Jeff nodded, with an understanding he didn't actually possess.

Harper gave them a bit of side-eye before continuing.

"Yeah. No. Nothing about… peanut brittle or the like. This dead old man became *really* dead, like *skeleton*-dead, right in front of these men."

"Is that true, Officer?" Tom asked.

Kelton nodded so vigorously, his hat flew off his head.

"You bet it is, Colonel. We seen it happen! One minute, this dead guy was walking right for us, arms upraised, all kinds of menacing. Ain't that right, Larry?"

"Sure is, Kelton," Larry said, grateful Kelton used his last name correctly.

"Next, he turned into a pile o' bones, like something you woulda seen in anatomy class," Kelton said excitedly.

"Man, did I love anatomy," Jeff added with a sigh. Paula hushed him.

Tom tipped his hat back on his forehead.

"I don't get it," he said, genuinely unsure. "You're telling me that not only is something raising the dead to use as weapons against American interests, but they're also reducing those *already* dead into something even *more* dead?"

Larry and Kelton nodded as one.

"That's about the size of it, Colonel," Harper offered. "As

we speak, we've got several squads of police officers out combing the grounds of this surprisingly large and deeply unexplored cemetery for answers. But so far, we've got zilch for our efforts."

"Well," Tom said, considering, "maybe it's high-time the police and the military join forces. Lord knows nothing bad ever comes of that."

"Right you are, Colonel," Paula said. "Back when I was training with Scotland Yard on investigative techniques, we found that—"

"For the love of God, Paula, would you please stop embarrassing me in front of the men? Apologies, Lieutenant. Colonel. My wife gets carried away sometimes, and forgets her place."

"Sorry everyone," Paula said with a grin. "Just my woman's head, getting in the way again."

"Here's what I suggest, gentlemen," Jeff said. "Colonel—you, me and the Lieutenant continue the search of the cemetery grounds for concrete answers for what's been happening here. The rest of you men stay behind, to protect my wife from these strange and terrible events. And from herself."

Kelton and Larry exchanged a look. They were dumb, but not *dumb*, you know?

"Ah… with all respect, wouldn't it make more sense if we all went out *together*? I mean, who knows what the hell we're going to find? Could be more trouble than you can handle on your own!"

Jeff's face turned an instant red from anger.

"Now see here—first of all, I'm a *captain* for Burbank Airways Unlimited. And that means I'm the highest ranking officer here."

Tom tilted his head at that.

"Ah… *actually*, I'm not sure that's—" he began, only for Jeff to roll right over him.

"Secondly, I'm a *taxpayer*. Which means I pay the salary

for both my local police and my national defense. So, technically, I'm your boss. All of you."

"He sure is the boss at home," Paula said cheerfully. "Especially for Mommy. Right, honey?"

Jeff winked at her and kept going.

"The point being, gentlemen, this is simply the best plan we've got."

Harper, Kelton, Larry, and Edwards all exchanged knowing looks.

"Sounds about right to me," Harper offered.

"I'm not positive—" Tom began, but was once again cut off.

"Good. Then it's settled. Now let's get out there and show these space bastards the what-for," Jeff said. "Damn space bastards."

Kelton and Larry looked at each other and shrugged.

"C'mon, boys," Paula said with a bright tone. "Show a married lady a good time. I may even let you film it."

She swished away with aplomb, the two patrolmen right on her heels.

"All right, men," Jeff said, turning on the flashlight he had with him. "Let's get out there and take care of these space bastards."

He marched off into the growing mist and gloom of the Burbank evening, with Tom and Harper close behind.

CHAPTER
TWENTY-TWO

THE THING that had been Daniel Clay shuffled through the overgrown underbrush of the Burbank cemetery.

The beast no longer had thoughts, not of his own, at any rate. Now, he was simply a vessel for the greater wishes of the Klezmers and the personal whims of those that controlled him.

Also, recipes.

Now that his mind was effectively wiped of any of the facets that had made him Inspector Clay, it turns out that the human brain made for a wonderful receptacle for all sorts of data. Really, for anything that Tanna (*and* Eros, but mostly Tanna) felt deserved a spot. And, in this case, that meant recipes.

Like every sentient being everywhere, Tanna harbored secret goals, to rise above and beyond her current station. Goals she believed would lead to her eventual happiness.

If I may take a moment to reflect here, there's something to be said about the universality of these dreams. If only we were better able to recognize this desire in others, we would perhaps be better equipped to find the empathy and grace that would lead to true happiness, everywhere.

But dreams are dreams. And this is reality.

As for Tanna, her dreams were simple in the end: To have the number-one rated cooking show in all of the known cosmos. She felt (rightly) that the consumption of food was perhaps the one universal constant. And that every creature had a right to food that tasted *good*.

Tanna also knew that there were trillions upon trillions of thinking creatures out there that fancied themselves to be "foodies" and, as such, were game to try new and different flavor profiles, new combinations they had never considered, and to dare themselves to experience culinary adventure!

On every interplanetary assignment on which Tanna found herself, she made a point to collect as many local recipes as she could, as well as gathering seed samples for the local grown fruits and vegetables.

To her way of thinking, if she presented herself as the first *truly* intergalactic chef, it would drive up interest in her show tenfold, maybe more. After all, 'standing out' was important in this field, which, culinary achievement aside, was show business in the end.

Tanna was also considering cooking fully in the nude. Which she assumed would drive up ratings as well, even though her producing partner raised valid questions about the sterility of food prep if she were naked.

Regardless of all that, Tanna had, at this point, gathered well over ten million different recipes from across the galaxy. As a result, her data banks were running out of room. So when the blank minds of the reanimated dead became available, it seemed to her that it would be a waste of resources NOT to use them for data storage.

A girl had to be resourceful, after all.

As the resurrected monster Clay bumbled his way towards his hidden mission, the ingredients list for wonton duck soup, creme brûlée, and Flacking Fur Frothing Foam (something from a planet in the Andromeda system) ran through the halls of his empty mind, making use of the blank space therein.

As he ambled through the headstones and monuments, he was joined by his counterpart, the Ghoul Woman, teeth bared, arms extended in a permanently-menacing way. Her mind too was full, but rather than recipes, it was stuffed to the gills with sports statistics.

Turns out Tanna, in addition to interstellar cuisine, was also a nut for *flugerball*, the primary sport on Klezmer. In flugerball, teams of twelve squared off against each other in an oval-shaped area. The teams then competed by throwing metallic "flugger" balls (that were all set aflame, mind you) at each other's heads. The flugerballs would explode their targets' heads upon impact.

After said explosion, the flugerball would then automatically extinguish its flame, position itself atop of the now-empty neck, implant electronic diodes into the body, all to be controlled by the opposing team.

The team with the last member standing was declared the winner.

Those that suffered the fate of the exploding head had their personalities and memories swiftly recorded by the flugerball, and were able to live out the rest of their lives, running their headless body from within the artificial reality the flugerball created.

It was *very* popular.

Klezmers were absolutely crazy about it, and the athletes were held in extremely high regard, especially as disembodied flugerball heads. (The number of times those players got married *after* the fact of losing their natural heads would just about make your own head spin.)

In any event, Tanna wasn't any different from her planet mates in this regard. She was wild about the game and enjoyed keeping records on every match, throughout league play, for study later.

She was convinced there were quantifiable *patterns* to the data that would suggest what teams would ultimately win out in a season. And to identify those players who were just in it to get their heads knocked off.

All that data was now residing within the brain of the Ghoul Woman, rattling against the interior of her skull like a little flugerball all its own.

She strode alongside the lumbering Clay, heading towards a dreaded purpose, with nothing but stats of active decapitations and various chip dip recipes to keep them company.

Kelton leaned against the hood of his patrol car, amazed to watch Paula Trent do intricate repair work on the engine with naught but two hairpins, a flashlight, a coat hanger and the bottle of moonshine Kelton kept on hand for 'emergencies.'

"Okay, Officer Kelton," Paula said, straightening herself up and wiping her hands against each other as she did, "I think I've managed to increase your horsepower output by a factor of three. I should've been able to coax five out of this baby, but, you know how it is… you can only use the tools ya got. Am I right?"

She smiled a smile that smiled more than any smile Kelton had ever seen.

"Ahhh… sure thing, Mrs. Trent. Thanks for taking a look at it," was the best he was able to manage.

"No problem. I like working on engines. Helps me relax. I'm so busy finishing the mountainside sculpture that I really need something to take my mind off it from time to time. Plus, you know… worried about Jeff and all. But what do I know? I'm only a woman!"

There were about a million things Kelton wanted to ask at the moment, like 'tell me about the mountainside sculpture', but then Larry came running in, panicked as always.

"Christ, Larry, not now, okay?" Kelton said with annoyance.

"But Kelton... it's Clay!!"

Kelton's jaw dropped to the ground. Literally. He had it shot off during the war and it was replaced by a prosthetic that could just snap in and out.

He picked it up, wiped it off, quickly stuffed it back into his mouth before Paula could see and turned to Larry with disbelief.

"What are you talking about? Inspector Clay is dead!"

"Not anymore, he ain't! He's here! With some crazy-looking woman with a waist smaller that seems reasonably healthy!"

There was a deep, inhuman growl from ahead the trees and there, like a bad moon rising, was the former Inspector Clay, face twisted into an ugly snarl, fists opening and closing like vices.

"Good Jumpin' Jehoshaphat, Kelton! What are we gonna do?" Larry Larry exclaimed, terror running through him like that time he tried the "Incandescent Fireball of Death" hot sauce on a dare last summer.

Kelton didn't have a single idea.

(There was a reason he had never advanced beyond patrolman in his nearly ten years on the force. A leader he was not.)

"I dunno, Larry! But we'd better figure it out before it's too late!"

Paula stepped up, a lug wrench in her hands, looking as cool as Christmas.

"Step aside, boys. I may only be a woman, but I got this," she said, gritting her teeth as she moved forward, using the cadence taught to her by the sword masters of Japan.

But a lug wrench was not a katana, no matter how skilled Paula was.

With Kelton and Larry watching in wonder, she swung the damn thing like a baseball bat, whacking the undead Clay right in the gut. It had little to no effect, likely a combination of Clay's natural bulk and the lack of working nerve endings.

But Paula hadn't given up when she soloed up K2, and she wasn't about to give up now.

With the two patrolmen cowering in the metaphorical corner and watching with wide eyes, Paula did a pirouette (courtesy of the Moscow Ballet), and used her momentum to slug Clay right in the head with the wrench.

It landed with a dull thud and Clay's unseeing eyes crossed, then uncrossed, then crossed again.

"Holy smokes, Mrs. Trent!" Kelton cried. "Look out!"

All Kelton did, however, was serve to distract Paula, whose focus was legendary; she once umpired an entire Wimbledon tournament by herself without a break.

She turned to look at Kelton, and that was the opening Clay needed. Swinging a fist the size of a side of beef, he clocked her, sending her flying and knocking her out.

"C'mon, Larry! We gotta do something!" Kelton said, screwing his courage to whatever sticking place he had left.

He and Larry leapt to their feet to defend Paula, but they were too late. The Ghoul Woman, unseen in all the chaos, had crept up behind them. As they moved to help, she grabbed them both by the sides of their heads and knocked them together like maracas.

The two police officers went down in a heap like forgotten sacks of old laundry that somehow has found themselves sitting on the side of a major highway, with people asking 'how did they get there?' And 'someone *must* have put it there' but no one actually doing anything to pick up said laundry and take it to the cleaners or the dump or the Goodwill or *somewhere* other than the side of the road.

With the cops down for the count, Clay scooped Paula Trent in his arms like a plaything and tossed her over his shoulder.

Soon, the odd little trio of Clay, the Ghoul Woman and Paula were gone, vanished into the mist and mire of the cemetery, shuffling through towards a mysterious goal known only to their alien overlords

It appeared as if there was nothing to save Paula now, not even had she been able to awaken and offer the secret to her award-winning recipe for Thanksgiving Ducking Trout, a dish known only to her. (It involved caramel, pink Himalayan salt, and fresh duck straight from the butcher. Curiously, there was no trout, nor any fish of any kind, in the recipe. When asked about that odd curiosity when she appeared on a local newscast after receiving a blue ribbon for her signature dish, Paula had said "I just like the word 'trout.' Isn't it fun?" There was no record of the reporter offering a reply to that opinion.)

The dark clouds in the night sky covered the moon, and soon, the cemetery was shrouded in darkness with only the faintest sound of lumbering footsteps to signal that anything had been there at all.

CHAPTER
TWENTY-THREE

Tom stumbled in the dark over a root. Or a stump. Or a grave marker. Or something. He muttered a curse under his breath. This was not the environment for Tom. He knew that as sure as he knew all of Gene Kelly's tap routines by heart.

He had never been much of a field officer, truth be told. Even when he was in Korea, it wasn't his combat skills that got him noticed and promoted. It was his ability to take care of things in triplicate. The army loved paperwork. Way more than just about anything else. More than guns and green clothing. Everything was paperwork: Forms for food, forms for fighting, forms for freight, forms for more forms (they ran out of those a lot, as you'd guess).

And Tom was terrific at it.

He'd fill out those little bastards like they were copies of the goddamn Magna Carta and sent them on their merry way. He was *efficient*, was Tom. Probably somehow related to his skill as a dancer. Gotta think fast, move faster, and get the thing done before it's too late.

In point of fact, the last time Tom had found himself "in the field" was on a required training exercise, wherein he managed to set off a landmine that he hadn't even stepped on and blew up a tank in the process. No one was inside at the time, thank heavens.

The sergeant in charge of said exercise said that in his twenty-eight years in the military, he had never seen anything like it. He followed that by promptly asking Tom to never come back.

So needless to say, Tom wasn't the most comfortable roughing it, as it were. He preferred the quiet of Pentagon hallways and the hushed whispers that followed him as he tap-tap-tapped his way along.

Even getting the assignment to take down the saucers as they buzzed D.C. had been a major surprise. Tom suspected that there may have been a bit of dirty dealing to get him out there. Word was his office (a Pentagon corner, with a window that crested two sides and thus, highly coveted) had been marked for a hostile takeover by some junior officers, and they had somehow made the assignment happen.

Regardless of who did it and why, Tom found himself now trudging through a truly dank and miserable place. And listen, he knew he didn't have a ton of experience with California, Los Angeles or show business, but this sure didn't seem like the "dream factory" other people made it out to be.

For one thing, the sheer acreage of this cemetery was staggering. How far could it stretch? It felt like the Pacific must be right next door, for Christ's sake.

Plus, he wasn't really caring for the company he was keeping on this little quest.

Lieutenant Harper was dour and sour, like some kid's face after drinking unsweetened lemonade. As they trudged along, Harper complained… A LOT… about the police force, his pension, his parking spot, his pronounced, early-receding hairline.

It was a bit exhausting, to be honest.

Then there was Jeff Trent.

Good *lord*, could the man talk. It was endless, really. A

stream of anecdotes and invectives. About his airline. His co-pilot. His house. And his wife.

Paula came up often and every time she did (which must've been every 3.5 seconds), Tom felt himself bristle.

Why on earth would any woman, let alone one as accomplished and as alluring as she, waste her time on a blowhard like Jeff Trent?

Tom couldn't figure it out.

He hadn't ever had much luck with the ladies, truthfully. He was, by nature, a bit on the shy side, and the only real skill he had was the tapping. Hard as it may be to believe, introducing yourself as a hoofer *wasn't* the magnet for the fairer sex as one might wish.

If he could only get Paula alone, talk to her, plainly and openly, about what her presence did to him and what an incredible impression she had already made on his heart.

But who was he kidding? He didn't even know Paula Trent, not really. And even if he did, what was he going to do? Sweep her off her feet (assuming she even *wanted* something like that, which was far from a guarantee), right out from under the nose of her handsome commercial airline pilot of a husband?

Tom thought the chances were unlikely.

And yet... he couldn't get her off of his mind. So lost in thought was Tom that, as he continued blindly following the men before him, he failed to notice a low-hanging tree branch.

He took two more steps and...

...WHAM!

Right into it he went, quickly tumbling like a house of cards in a stiff breeze.

Stars blinked and twinkled in Tom's vision and he felt two pairs of hands hoist him up by the arms.

"You all right there, partner?" Tom heard Harper say.

"LOOOOOOOOOOOOOOOOOW *bridge!*" Jeff brayed, finding it profoundly funny. He nearly doubled over, he was laughing so hard.

"Yup… that's… that's a good one, Mr. Trent," Tom managed to eke out, taking off his

hat and rubbing the spot where he ran into the tree.

"Seriously, you okay, Colonel?" Jeff said, with something that managed to sound minimally like concern. "Where'd you go there? Looked like you were contemplating something serious."

Tom wanted to say he was picturing Paula in a general's uniform, nodding in approval while she smoked a large cigar, watching him do a tap dance wearing nothing but his shoes, a smile, and his aviator glasses.

But he figured that wouldn't go over well.

So instead he said—

"—Oranges."

It was the first thing that popped into his head.

Harper and Trent exchanged a look.

"Oranges?" Harper repeated.

Tom felt himself go flush, like that time he had shown up for a dance gig without his shoes and had to make do with forks strapped to his bare feet.

"Uh. Yeah. Just… you know. California oranges. Why are they? Orange, I mean."

Blank stares came his way.

"And the word, you know? Nothing rhymes with it. What's that about?"

Harper opened his mouth to speak, but quite literally couldn't think of anything at all to say.

"That's a good point, Colonel," Trent said, stepping forward. "Thanks for bringing it up. But really we should focus on looking for those aliens—"

Now it was *Jeff's* turn to inadvertently walk right into an inanimate object that was obvious to anyone else standing nearby.

He went *smack* into the hull of the alien spacecraft, bouncing off it and hitting the deck hard.

Tom burst into laughter. He knew he shouldn't, but honestly, he just couldn't help himself.

"Dammit, Edwards," Jeff said as Harper helped him to his feet, "what the hell is so funny?"

Tom clammed up immediately, knowing he had crossed a line.

The two men were staring at him and were clearly waiting for an answer.

"Door hinge," Tom sputtered out.

"What?" Trent said incredulously.

Tom cleared his throat.

"Door hinge. If you say it fast, as if it's one word, it rhymes with 'orange.' Right?"

There was a silence that hung in the air, heavy and thick (which, incidentally, was how Harper liked his orange juice).

Tom pointed at the ship.

"Hey, look! Alien space invaders!"

Jeff harrumphed at that declaration.

"Easy now, Colonel. We don't know that for sure."

"Don't know what?" Tom responded, confused.

"That they're invaders. We don't have hard evidence of that."

"You mean... other than buzzing the capital of the United States, taking direct assault fire from our armed forces, robbing graves, hiding from our most sophisticated detection technology, and moving inexorably towards some nefarious purpose?"

Jeff and Harper considered those points.

"Yeah," Jeff said finally. "Other than that."

Tom felt his blood pressure rise and took a step towards Jeff (with what intent, he honestly wasn't sure), when Harper intervened.

"Fellas, let's not get lost in the weeds here," he said.

"I wouldn't say that," Jeff replied. "I think that overall, this cemetery is very well-kept."

Harper blinked twice.

"Right. What I'm saying is, how can we get *inside* this damned thing? I don't see a hatch, a door, a porthole, nothing that gives a hint on opening it up and getting in there," he said.

"Okay," Jeff said, rubbing his chin in a way that he was sure made him look like a professor of... well, *something*. "What about *this*?"

He pulled out his revolver and fired off three quick shots, one after the other. The bullets raced to the ship's hull, immediately bounced off, and went ricocheting all over the place.

One *just* whizzed past Tom's ear, missing him by inches. It lodged into a nearby headstone, the following epithet carved upon it... 'Good father, better husband, best son-of-a-gun bowler' with an exclamation it hadn't had previously.

"All right, hold your fire! We aren't going to shoot our way in!" Tom declared with frustration. "You're just going to get us killed!"

Jeff scoffed.

"I don't think so, Colonel. I'm a man of action. Can't help it if you're intimidated by that little bit of information."

Tom sighed heavily. He'd had enough of this. Stalking right past Jeff, he stared him dead in the eye.

Keeping eye contact, he strode over to a wide, marble gravestone, one laid into the earth.

Tom cleared his throat, stretched a bit, took out a handkerchief and did a quick bit of polishing on his taps.

Then he started to dance atop the tomb, a dance like he never had before, past injuries be damned. The other two stared in wonder and amazement. It was a dance no one on Earth had ever seen.

It turned out, like no one on any planet *anywhere* had ever seen.

...If you catch my drift.

Meanwhile, as all of this was unfolding, the three men had no idea they were being closely monitored by Eros, watching from the internal sensor screen in the cockpit.

The image was great.

Really first-rate video technology, high definition, surround-sound, with automatic color and balance correction.

"Tanna," Eros said excitedly, "get in here!"

After a moment, Tanna appeared in a robe, her hair in a towel.

"What is it, Eros? You know I was taking a shower. I needed it after being so close to all these corpses."

"Never mind that now!" Eros said impatiently, pointing at the monitor screen. "Look at this, for Klezmer's sake!"

Tanna rolled her eyes but did as asked.

There, kicking up a storm, was the human known as Colonel Tom Edwards. And that bastard was dancing as if his life depended on it!

Heels flying, toes tapping, body twisting, sweat pouring from his brow.

Tanna felt her insides warm up again. Those insides were getting a lot of action these days.

"What is this?" she demanded of Eros. "Ritual combat? Mating dance? Ritualized mating dance combat?"

Eros nodded.

"Exactly. Impressive, is it not?"

Watching as Tom leapt into the air once more, only to come down, feet ablaze, literally causing sparks as he tapped his way across the stone, Tanna nodded.

"*Very* impressive, I'd say," she purred, wondering if there was a way to get this human into private—*consultations* with herself and The Ruler. Now, *that* would be a mission to the stars.

"I think, given the effort they're making out there, they've earned the right to come into the interior of the ship. See what's happening inside. What do you say, Tanna?"

"I'm all for his coming inside," she said, slowly pulling the towel off of her head.

"Excellent," Eros said. "Then let it be so!"

He busied himself pressing various buttons and controls, while Tanna scurried out to make herself more presentable to their new guests.

—◆—

Tom's recital came to a close. He was panting, breathing heavily, and was drenched with sweat. He hadn't danced like that in a long time, let alone in a thick, wool military uniform.

He leaned over at the waist, hands on knees, trying to catch his breath. When Tom finally looked up, he saw Jeff nodding in wordless approval.

"That was... really something," he finally said. "I had no idea that part of military training included tap dance. How remarkable. How ingenious. How inspiring!"

He reached out to shake Tom's hand vigorously.

"Don't worry, Colonel. I understand now. Truly. And you won't find me challenging you again. I give you my word as a pilot, *and* as a member in good standing of the Leather-of-the-Month Club."

Before Tom could respond, Harper blurted out, "No, really, what the hell is happening here? 'Cause I don't get it. Not even a little bit."

"ALLOW ME TO SPEAK TO THAT, HUMAN!" came a booming voice from behind them.

The trio turned to see Eros and Tanna, uniforms immaculate, eyes shining with power, probably posing a little bit, if we were being fair.

"Come! We invite you to experience wonders the likes of which you've never seen! Never felt! Never experienced before! And indeed, will be the first humans in your history to have!"

Eros and Tanna stepped aside from their portal, beckoning the three men inside. Tom, Jeff, and Harper all exchanged looks. Did they dare enter? Did they continue their pursuit to the next point? And from there, where did it end? Did it just go on and on and on?

"C'mon," Tanna said. "Don't be afraid. We aren't going to eat you."

"Certainly not unprepared," Eros added helpfully.

Harper shook his head with determination.

"What choice do we have?" he said grimly.

"None," Tom replied. None at all."

Setting his jaw, he nodded.

"Let's go, men."

With their two hosts guiding the way, Army Colonel Tom Edwards, Airline Pilot Captain Jeff Trent, and Burbank Police Lieutenant John Harper stepped forward, becoming the first humans to ever set foot aboard a craft whose origin was not of this world.

Click-clacking their way into history.

CHAPTER
TWENTY-FOUR

ONCE INSIDE THE SPACECRAFT, the three humans were struck by how... *ordinary* it looked. No high-intensity diodes, no holographic screen projections, no self-aware robots busying themselves by bustling back and forth.

It kinda looked like an office. Like... a middle-of-downtown, Burbank-bland office. A couple of desks. One metal cabinet with some dials and blinking lights. A couple of rolling chairs. Nothing special.

Sure, everything was sleek and metallic, and there weren't many hard angles in the place, but still. Nothing that screamed "advanced technology."

"I gotta say," Jeff remarked, putting his hands on his hips, "I'm a little disappointed."

"Yeah," Harper concurred. "It doesn't exactly fit the profile, does it? I mean, this makes it seem like a good temp agency could take over this ship."

"Oh, that's where you would be *wrong*, Lieutenant Harper," a powerful voice called out.

The three men turned to see Eros of Klezmer, looking resplendent in his freshly-steamed uniform.

"Yes, indeed, gentlemen. We are aware of you all. Including you, Captain Jeff Trent, pilot and connoisseur of fine leather goods from across the American West. And you, Colonel Tom Edwards, whose true secret passion isn't tap dancing at all. But tap-dancing–while *knitting*."

The other two looked at Edwards.

He shrugged.

"It's relaxing."

"We make no judgments here, Earthman. Except in matters of intergalactic security!" Eros thundered with authority.

"What the hell does that mean?" Jeff shouted.

"I'll tell you!"

Eros strode forward, strutting like a flizzersnam (a very flamboyant bird of prey on Klezmer, known for its distinctive mating call, which, to human ears, would sound like a particularly thick, wet sneeze).

"It means that you earthlings are not to be trusted with the secrets of the universe! For you will only destroy yourselves and us in the process!"

"All right, all right," Tom said, raising his hands in a show of non-aggression, "let's ease it up on the hyperbole. In the dancing world, that's what we call a 'tapmeister.' Nobody wants to see that."

There was a moment of silence then.

"Who calls it that?" Harper asked incredulously.

"Dancers. People in the know."

"I don't think that's true."

"Neither do I," Jeff added.

"Well, neither of you are dancers, so what would you know about it anyway?" Tom countered, perhaps a touch defensively.

"I'm just saying… 'tapmeister' sounds made up," Harper said.

Jeff nodded.

"It does."

"Why would I make that up?"

"Well," Eros began, stepping forward, "…if I may?"

Jeff and Harper ceded the floor.

"We Klezmers have been monitoring Earth communications for the better part of several decades, as you reckon time. Never once have we encountered the term 'tapmeister,' lending credence to the theory of your fellows here that you, in fact, have invented that phrase as of this moment."

Tom's face turned a brilliant red, and his toes tapped twitchingly unbeknownst to himself.

"Yeah, well... *I'm* the only dancer here... so... yeah," as the best response he was able to manage.

"Okay," Jeff said, "let's move past this. There are sure to be hiccups in these first days of human / Kleenex relations."

"Klez*mer*," Eros corrected.

"*Gesundheit*," Harper offered, looking over to Tom. "Learned that in the war."

"What?"

"This is *irrelevant*, humans!" Eros shouted. "DOOM is coming for us all! And we cannot allow that to happen!"

'Explain it," Tom said carefully. "Explain it to us. So we can understand. Perhaps, if we did, we'd be able to help you stop this disaster from happening."

Eros shook his head. He knew it was nearly too late as it was. But... he decided it was better to share this information than keep it to himself.

"Very well," he started solemnly. "Let it be so."

He moved to one of the desk consoles and sat down, delicately crossing his legs as he did.

Jeff whistled softly himself. *That uniform sure looks awfully good*, he thought, settling in to listen to Eros.

"It began simply enough," Eros began... simply enough. "Man, though not much more advanced than the other primates of this word, learned that by mixing charcoal and bird guano together, you could light a spark that would eventually shake the foundations of the Earth itself.

Why would anyone have looked at bird droppings and thought 'Hmm. What can I do with *that*?' is beyond me, but here we are nonetheless.

What am I saying, gentlemen? I am saying that this is where *gunpowder* was born. Whose only purpose is to inflict harm on members of your own species. Gunpowder. You used it for pistols, rifles, then cannons. Each iteration growing more destructive, more powerful. Harder to undo.

Even turning this formula into something celebratory, like fireworks, has proven to be problematic. Fields, forests, homes... all set alight by this nonsensical display of explosives, as if the lights from the heavens above weren't enough for your small, petty minds. All of the cosmos is there for you to marvel at, but instead, you chose to blow things up to watch them go 'bang.'

Pathetic."

(It was at this moment that all three humans present opened their mouths to protest this, but two things happened: First, they realized Eros was right. Second, Eros just kept on rollin.')

"But from the firework came the dynamite. Then the hand grenade. From the hand grenade to the missile. From the missile to the *bomb*. Always finding new levels of destruction, of annihilation. It was never enough to *kill*. It had to be, how *much* can we kill? Isn't that your way, human? As much destruction as can be mustered, eh?

CLEAR THE BOARD!

That's what you like, you sickos.

But even TNT wasn't giving you enough bang for you buck, was it? You're like wastrels at a nude-only drinking establishment where the females of your species dance while growing increasingly bored as you throw money and demand more and more extremity!

So from TNT came the splitting of the atom! A fundamental element to the universal construction. With that splitting came nearly limitless energy, at tremendous cost. Balls of fire that are rivaled only by your sun. BUT–it was STILL not enough for you people!

From there, came an even *more* powerful weapon, the hydrogen bomb! With the force to end this world ten times over!

Surely, one would think—any rational, temperate, considering species would think anyway—that this weapon was the end of the line. What need more? How much further destruction could be *wrought* by one race of sentient, yet small-minded, creatures?

It's a good question. I'm glad you asked."

(No one asked.)

"*Solaronite.*

What's that, you ask in your small, pitiful voices?"

(Again…no one asked.)

"Solaronite is the most powerful force for destruction in the entirety of the universe. It is an element that literally *explodes* beams of light from stars into component parts, unleashing utterly unimaginable levels of power. Imagine that—light—*EXPLODING*.

There is nothing in existence that would be able to survive such an apocalyptic onslaught of slaughter!

How does it work, you ask?

(Probably goes without saying, but no question here either.)

Even a single use of solaronite would be enough to create a chain reaction, throughout *all the light in the universe*, making every *particle* a weapon the likes of which could destroy entire worlds in mere moments.

Humankind is already well down the path towards discovering solaronite, an element that has been banned throughout the galaxy by every intelligent, self-sustaining species. We cannot allow you to proceed in this unchecked, continuing ever-onward in an endless arms race that will only stop when complete catastrophe has befallen not only *you*, but every civilization and life form in all of the cosmos!

(Now, at this point, Tom *did* raise his hand to ask something...)

Oh, we *tried*. You can bet your life on that. We tried! Eight previous plans, in point of fact! But you have left us with no other choice! Humankind's continued insistence on ignorance, on being absolutely unwilling to engage with anyone other than themselves, is simply breathtaking to behold!

(...but it wasn't that.)

So now... here we are! We have been ignored at your own peril! We have indeed unleashed Plan **9**, the most *dreaded* of plans upon you all, to teach this lesson: Life is precious, *all* life, not just man's! Respect must be paid! Respect must be given!

And if that respect is to be granted willingly, then we must avail ourselves of whatever means we have at our disposal to take that respect!

You will not be allowed to bring about the armageddon of all life on Earth and everywhere else for good measure. Some justice *must* be done. And if we Klezmers are the only ones willing to carry that torch, then carry it we will! Alone, if necessary, but never with a hanging head. Indeed, we *thrive* under such expectations. It is for this very reason that the Klezmers are the envy of the greater community of civilized societies, space-faring and otherwise, from each corner of the universe.

I see you trembling, humans."

(No one was trembling.)

"As you should! You have brought this fate upon yourselves. If only you had listened to reason. If only you had heeded the better angels of your nature. But, no. Why do that, when it's more fun to blow things up!

Yes, you're *right* to cower."

(No one was cowering.)

"This is the endgame that you have played yourselves into, like a game of *splutterknox!*"

(SIDE NOTE: *Splutterknox* was the name of a very popular strategy game amongst the Klezmer people. The short version: players battle for territory on a large game board, using only the force of their... gas emissions... to knock down game pieces. Protective masks and goggles were sold separately.)

"So, we Klezmers willingly step into the breach, for we cannot sit idly by as the universe is brought to ruin by a species as small and underdeveloped as human beings. It's not an easy burden to bear, I can tell you that. But we are a hardy race, born amongst the cold, sharp mountains of Klezmer Prime, where freezing rain falls for twelve of the fifteen months of the year. Where we are taught to climb the poisonous *slickalack* tree before we are taught to walk!"

(SIDE NOTE: The *sickalack* tree wasn't actually poisonous. It was just that most Klezmers were allergic to its seed nuts. But they ate them anyway. Go figure.)

"We will not fail! We will not falter! We will stop this curse of humanity from spreading throughout space like cold sores at a summer camp! Rest assured, life *will* be saved. And we will do whatever is necessary to make sure of that!"

Eros finished, panting, eyes aglow.

"Sorry," Jeff said, scratching at his right ear. "I got lost in the middle there. What was that?"

It was said later that birds for miles around scattered from their nests and the trees they called home, so powerful was the scream of frustration that Eros let loose at that moment.

After things had settled down slightly, Tom tried raising a hand again.

"Excuse me, Mr.—?"

"You may address me as *EROS*, human!"

The three human men exchanged a look.

"Eros? You mean… *Cupid*?" Tom asked with a smirk.

"Why do you say that, Colonel?" said Eros. "I don't understand."

"If I remember my Greek mythology correctly, *Eros* was the son of Aphrodite. He was the god of love. He was Cupid."

Jeff burst out laughing, nearly doubling over.

"You mean *this* guy is Cupid?"

"I'm not sure that I'm exactly saying *that*, but—" Tom began only to be cut off by Eros himself.

"Wait a moment—what is this 'Cupid' you are speaking of?"

"Cupid is a human mythological figure. A creature who induces love in his subjects."

"By dressing like a baby with stupid little wings on his back!" Jeff barked out like a seal, the laughter fully turned into guffaws as he did so.

"That doesn't… I mean… it doesn't sound *so* bad," Eros said, scrambling for dignity.

"It's damn ridiculous, is what it is," Jeff said. "A fat little baby, wearing nothing but a diaper, with some toy bow he uses to shoot… I dunno… *love* arrows at people. He floats around, like, on clouds or something, doesn't he?"

Harper nodded in concurrence.

"He sure does."

"Hard to be afraid of a tiny baby, Mr. *Eros*," Jeff cackled.

Tom was silent for a moment through this, considering something. Finally, he spoke. "Eros, what is the lifespan of a typical Klezmer? In Earth years?"

Eros, red as a beet, struggled to come to himself again.

"It depends, I suppose. The effects of Klezmer gravity are very different from such effects on Earth. Our planet's orbit is also significantly wider and longer than yours. And if you factor in medical advances, improvements made to the quality of food and nutrients—"

"Oh, Christ, out with it, already!" Harper commanded.

"It could be as long as several thousand Earth years," Eros said, with a shrug. "Give or take."

"So—it *is* possible," Tom said, almost to himself.

"What, Colonel? What's 'possible'?" Harper asked. Jeff was still chortling to himself over in the corner.

"Think about it. If the Klezmers had visited Earth in the past—"

"We have," Eros offered with some defiance.

"—then it's likely that they were viewed by earlier human civilizations as something akin to gods. In fact, it's likely that humans took the names of those alien creatures that they had encountered and incorporated them into their own myths."

"Wait a minute," Harper said, rubbing his eyes with confusion and exhaustion, "you're saying that the Klezmers here might be—"

"—the source of all human mythology. Well, maybe not *all*. But *some*. The Greeks at least. This could rewrite an enormous amount of our history!"

Tom's eyes glowed with possibility of what this could mean, the papers he could write, the promotions he could receive, the interpretative dances he could create!

As for Eros, the enormity of what was being suggested was finally striking him. And he found it to his liking.

"You're saying that I might be an essential part of the history of this backwater world? That I may have wielded unknown influence for generations of humanity, sculpting their path forward in ways that I hadn't ever suspected?"

He was a bit lost in the dream.

"Sure," Tom said. "I mean, it's at least *possible* that—"

"—that *Eros* here was mistaken for the god of love?" a female voice asked incredulously from behind them.

The three human men and Eros all turned to see Tanna standing there, looking like a million *klezblocks*.

(SIDE NOTE: *Klezblocks* were a unit of measurement for their cheese currency.)

"That seems unlikely, in the extreme. Why, the most ol' Eros knows about love is when he offers up his book of rules late at night when the lights are low. Isn't that right, Eros?" she said with a wicked little grin.

That deep red color came back to Eros' face again.

"Hey, listen… regulatory books deserve attention too," he said with some small sense of pride.

"Who are *you*?" Jeff asked with some renewed interest.

"I am Tanna, director prefect of this mission. Subordinate to Eros, hard as that may be to believe. Here to do my part to stop an intergalactic war from breaking out."

"War? What war?" Tom asked with genuine confusion.

"The war that is inevitable, human. The war that will span across the stars!"

Jeff sighed.

"Here we go again."

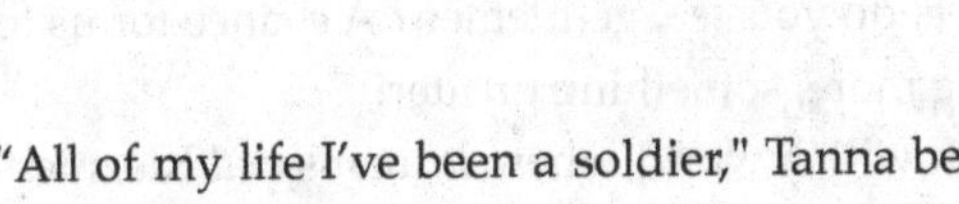

"All of my life I've been a soldier," Tanna began, running her hands along the smooth lines of her uniform. "Fighting for the betterment of my people, the survival of our species. That was the only thing that mattered to me. Well, that and my cooking-and-cookware empire I plan on building. But for centuries of your Earth years, I have travelled across this vast galaxy, sometimes with Eros, sometimes not, if I got the lucky draw on the assignment board.

And I have seen that the *one* universal constant is *war*.

Every intelligent species succumbs to its temptations, at one time or another. It seems impossible to avoid!

These people live on *this* land and they don't want to share it with *those* people over there. That is the essence of what war is. Preserving your own and the prevention of others from taking it.

It seems that this is the price we must pay as cognizant creatures: Conflict. There's no way around but *through*. War is the growing pain that civilizations endure before they come to enlightenment. Too often, even *after* that fact, it still happens. More than you weak humans would believe

Perhaps that is the fate designed for all of us by the great *Klezmerino!*"

(SIDE NOTE: *Klezmerino* is the name of the chief deity of the Klezmer people, a god or spiritual force that lives in a circular cloud that covers the planet at its equator. There has been persistent meteorological speculation that those clouds are just clouds, but... you know. Folks believe what they want to believe.)

"Regardless of fate, divine plans, and the whims of the gods, it is the *duty* of every intelligent creature to fight *against* that fate! Surely there are greater designs for all of us, rather than simply fall into endless conflict and combat, an unending cycle that burns and perpetuates itself throughout universal history!

This is a chance, do you see, gentlemen? A chance for us to achieve something more, something greater!

Imagine, if you will, a world where humans *and* Klezmers *and* Marfolans *and* Xenotops *and* Plantagens *and* Sniddlysnoos *and*—"

(SIDE NOTE: At this point, Tanna continued listing the names of various sentient races. This list lasted for the better part of an hour, as humans reckon time. In the interest of brevity, the list has been cut off after those named above. For further information on those space-faring species... well... honestly... you're not ready for that yet.)

"—a coalition of those forces would be truly unstoppable! No conflict we couldn't conquer, no disease we couldn't eliminate. Think of the scientific achievement! Think of the resources we could share! Think of the future we could build!

An intergalactic coalition of uniform advancement, peace, and sexual satisfaction the likes of which has never been contemplated before!"

(SIDE NOTE: At this point, Jeff Trent opened his mouth to speak, but was silenced by Tom, who quietly and gently shook his head 'No.')

"I beg of you: Think of your people. Think of yourselves. Think of the *children*! There is so much we could do together, if only we allowed for the possibility! Let us be bold! Let us be brave! And let us steer towards a bright and better future... *together!*"

Tanna finished, eyes closed, arms extended. It was all very dramatic.

There was silence for a moment as the assembled males took in what she had said.

It was Eros that finally broke the spell she had cast.

"Anyway, we'll blow you up if you don't do what we want."

"LET ME ASK YOU SOMETHING," Officer Larry said, as he and Kelton leaned against their patrol car. Since the lieutenant had headed off with that army colonel and airplane pilot, and Mrs. Trent being kidnapped, there really wasn't much for the rest of the cops to do.

They were all kind of just... flittering about, pretending to look busy. They'd been over this cemetery with a fine-tooth comb (literally. Larry took the comb out of his pocket at one point and ran it along the ground, just in case there were some small clues that otherwise wouldn't have been spotted).

But now these guys were mostly bored. And confused.

It occurred to Kelton that they should have been doing more to track down Mrs. Trent after she had been scooped up by that weird, dead, shuffling Inspector Clay, but they had lost them in the mist and darkness of the cemetery.

As the ranking officer (and wasn't *that* a sobering thought), Kelton didn't think it was the wisest decision to send all the men out into the wild searching for a creature that was also a former officer. It felt... well, disrespectful somehow.

Plus—and this was going to be a real sticking point at the

department meeting later that week—no one had thought to bring flashlights.

Kelton had been considering this: Most of the Burbank police force were wandering around this old graveyard, for what seemed like several days at this point. So what the hell was happening in town?

Looting? Riots? People running lights and stop signs with impunity? The possibilities were endless.

Kelton had to admit, after being on the "right" side of the law for so long, the prospect of going rogue kind of appealed to him. He fantasized about having a big ol' motorcycle. Something he could rev up so loudly that it would shake the window, some bitchin' babe on the back, arms around his waist, dressed in leather from top to bottom, the only law he kept was the law of the road...

Yeah...

But there were several problems with that scenario:

One—Kelton was allergic to leather.

Like... catastrophically so. No gloves, no jackets, even his *shoes* needed to be built out of something else. When he was exposed to leather, his skin would break out in hives that itched something *awful*. No one had been able to determine *why* exactly he had developed this condition. It had been speculated that it was psychosomatic and was related to the time his father ran with the bulls in Pamplona and never returned, instead "marrying" one of the bulls in a strange ceremony that was considered legal in at least three small Asian countries and parts of Nevada, never to be seen again.

Two—the motorcycle was a non-starter.

Kelton had tried to learn how to ride, but because he was missing all the bones in his inner ear, he has no sense of balance. At all. Physical therapy had helped him keep his feet (both literally and figuratively) in the intervening years, but man... you sat him atop a bike and the poor bastard just fell over. Instantly. Even with his feet on the ground as he straddled it. So his hog-riding days were over before they began.

Three—Kelton couldn't *abide* arms wrapped around his waist.

For one thing, it just drove him crazy. If he can't see who it is, then *how does* he know who it is? Just 'cause someone *says* they're putting their arms around you doesn't mean that it's *that* person when the time actually comes! Could be anyone! For another thing, Kelton had a hard time breathing when any kind of weight or pressure was put on his abdomen. This was another case of doctors not being able to exactly determine the source of this condition, but Kelton was pretty sure what it was:

When he was nine (the year his father ran with…and *off* with…the bulls) that story became fodder for the rumor mill in the school. And a couple of kids had cornered Kelton in the school library, forced him to lay down on his back, and proceeded to stack every book they could find that had anything to do with bulls, cows, farming, hell, even *cheeseburgers*, right down on his belly.

He was buried in bull books.

Tough to get over that.

Kelton was reflecting on all of these things when Larry nudged him in the ribs.

"What?" Kelton said impatiently.

"I said 'Let me ask you something'," Larry repeated, annoyed.

"Christ, fine. What is it?"

"Okay," Larry said, gathering himself. "What would you think about me changing my name?"

"What? Why do you want to do that?"

Larry shrugged, embarrassed.

"Well, you know how it is, Kelton. I mean, *you've* got it easy. 'Kelton.' Plain. Simple. Nice, hard 'kay' sound in there. It's a good name. But me? 'Larry Larry.' First of all, as you well know, people never pronounce it correctly—"

Kelton didn't know that, but it didn't seem like the time to bring it up.

"—and second of all, I really feel like a name change might be what I need to get my *real* career going."

That hung in the air like a pregnant storm cloud, as Larry was clearly waiting for a follow-up question.

Kelton swallowed hard.

"Gee, Larry, what's your... 'real' career?"

"I'm glad you asked. I've been wanting to talk with you about it. I think it will interest you."

"Okay, kid," Kelton said, already deeply regretting taking part in this conversation, "hit me. What's going on?"

"Again, as you know, I've long had an interest in game shows."

Kelton didn't know that either, but it seemed unlikely that would matter to the proceedings.

"Uh-huh," he managed to say.

"And I really, truly think, that with the right name change, I could *finally* find myself in the mix to become a game show *announcer.*"

He said that last part with all the pride of a Nobel Prize winner.

"You want to be the announcer? Not the host?"

Larry shook his head with so much enthusiasm, Kelton was afraid it was going to come flying off.

"Heck, no! Any old body can be a host. That doesn't require any kind of skill! Just gotta smile and usher people from one part of the stage to another. But when you're the *Announcer*... that's where the *real* juice lies."

His eyes gleamed with passion and maybe just a touch of insanity.

"As the announcer, *you're* the force that dictates what happens next. You're responsible of pronouncing contestants' names correctly, introducing sponsors, *saying the name of the show*! *That's* what people remember! Not some clowny host who makes a fool of himself on national television every week like a performing monkey! No, my friend, *announcing* is where the actual power lies. But obviously, no one is going to hire an announcer named 'Larry Larry.' They never get it right, you know? So I was thinking, what if I changed my name to something *stronger*, something that has hard edges to it. Like Rod Roddington. Or Butch McButchers. Or Steve Stallion. I mean, I think any of those could work, it's just a matter of deciding what I want my brand to be, right? You gotta consider that these days, your *brand*. You're never *not* selling. Always have to be primed, always ready to *go*. And I think a name like that could do wonders for me in this regard. I mean, let's be honest: 'Larry Larry' has a certain kind of poetry to it, gotta thank my folks for that. It's not like they weren't trying to give me the best chance that they could, but it just doesn't ring out, like a hammer on an anvil! And *that's* what you want a stage name to do. It needs to pound its way into the viewers' souls, embedded like recessed carpentry! Something you'll never forget! I swear to you, Kelton, I get the right name, and I'll book one of those gigs. And then it's 'adios' to the Burbank Police Department. Heck, it's 'adios' to *Burbank*! I'll get out of this town. Make it down the road to Hollywood proper. Maybe even New York! I mean, sky's the limit, right? So dream big: London. Bangkok. Shanghai. Sydney, Evansville! Who knows where I could go with a new name? Just gotta get it right, just gotta make the smart choice. Once I do that, I can do anything at all!"

Larry, finished, breathing heavily, a touch of sweat glistening on his brow. He was looking out deep into the middle distance, seeing nothing but a glorious future wherein he becomes the world's greatest game show… *announcer*.

Kelton tipped his hat back on his forehead. He'd never heard Larry talk this way, although he'd long suspected Larry had it in him to incomprehensibly rant. And boy, he proved that to be true. Nodding slightly, Kelton felt an odd sense of pride for the young patrolman.

He was growing up.

Kelton reached out a hand and put it on Larry Larry's

shoulder, the contact bringing the poor sap back down to earth.

"Here's what I think, kid," Kelton began, "anything you want, you can do. I really do believe that. But, in my admittedly very limited experience, I would say that names like 'Rod Roddington' lend themselves more towards the... ah... *adult* industry, than the professional announcing profession."

Larry stared at Kelton, then shrugged.

"I could do that too."

Before Kelton could respond to such a casual admittance of sexual prowess, everyone dropped what they were doing (literally. Things in hand—guns, notepads, coffee cups, a crowbar, strangely, hats, whatever—all fell to the ground at the same time with a 'THUD') to witness the appearance of the Ghoul Woman, still dressed in her witchy blacks, hands raised as talons, face menacing, teeth bared.

"Holy Christ, here we go again," Kelton exclaimed.

Larry was staring at her, gobsmacked.

"You know," he offered, "she's got the look. Maybe her and Rod Roddington could shoot a little scene together. What do you think?"

His earnestness was both endearing and disturbing.

Kelton was about to respond, but there was a low growl and creepy moaning. Looking up... the Ghoul Woman was gone!

Everyone looked around in wonder, but she was nowhere to be seen.

Kelton furrowed his brows.

Seemed kinda pointless to him. Like a scene in a movie that didn't advance the plot nor reveal any character details of any kind.

All of the cops assembled stopped groveling in abject fear and began picking up the things they had dropped to the ground. Even a couple of the donuts were retrieved, after having been deemed to have been only on the ground too briefly to matter.

"Well, jeez, Kelton," Larry said, "what do you make of that?"

But Kelton had no idea. No idea at all.

Whatever it was and whatever that woman portended, he knew it wasn't going to be good.

Plus, all he could see in his mind was her and Larry going downtown on each other.

And that was the stuff of nightmares.

CHAPTER
TWENTY-SIX

JEFF WAS DETERMINED that mankind wasn't going to go out like a weak little lamb crying for its mother. No way. Not on his watch.

Besides, Jeff liked lambs and he had always felt like they got the short end of the stick in the cute animal rankings.

Yeah, sure, kittens, puppies, and bear cubs, they get all the glory. But really, a sweet lamb is as cute as anything!

"We're not going to sit by and watch you aliens just take us out, you can be sure of that!" he said with a defiant tone. "You're going to find that earthlings are more than you can handle, I promise you that!"

Eros laughed, cold and icy. And too long. Like… *really* too long. Like… it was nearly *five full* minutes of laughing. On paper, that doesn't read like much, granted. But imagine standing there, listening to someone laughing for five damn minutes. Try it sometime.

Time it. See how it feels.

It's an eternity, honestly.

After Eros finally took a steady breath, eyes watering from all the guffawing, Jeff jumped right back in.

"What's so funny, space-man? You don't think humans are up to the challenge?"

"Oh, I can assure you, you're *not*," Eros replied, cocky as the day is long. "You're no match for our technology. You can barely even fly, let alone traverse the stars! The best of your weapons don't even make a scratch on our vehicles. How could you be expected to match up with our forces?"

"Be careful where you're stepping, Klezmer," Tom chimed in. "I grant you, we didn't make much of a showing this first go-round. But if we've proven anything as a species, it's that we don't give up. And we come back in the most annoying, bothersome way we can come up with. All of our history backs that up."

Eros considered. That point was hard to argue against.

"Regardless, we'll conquer you in less time than saying… *baclaclavarionsnooklesnaxationlesssupgerlash*."

The three humans shared a confused look.

"Maybe not the best example, Eros," Tanna said, rolling her eyes.

"What did you say?" Harper asked, genuinely interested.

"*Baclaclavarionsnooklesnaxationlesssupgerlash*."

Eros stood stone faced and let them soak it in.

"And what is that?"

"It's the word we use to describe the sensation of something taking less time than you think."

More blank stares.

"What? It's pretty clear," Eros said, suddenly self-conscious.

"Yeah, but…" Harper offered, "wouldn't it be just easier to say, 'this won't take as much time as you think'?"

Eros sputtered at that.

"But… we have a word!"

Jeff shook his head.

"I dunno. Gotta agree with my colleagues here. Seems unnecessarily complex. But maybe that's just me."

Eros was fuming.

"I always thought it was kind of stupid myself," Tanna added.

"That's not helping, Tanna," Eros pouted. "But maybe *this* will!"

He pressed a button, turning on a video monitor in the ship. The image flickered to life like a struggling candle, revealing the exterior of the ship and the grounds beyond.

And there, lurching into frame, was Clay, carrying his arms, the limp and unconscious form of Paula Trent!

"No! Paula!" Jeff exclaimed. "What are you doing to her, you animals?"

"Why, we haven't done anything. *Yet*." Eros said confidently. But the time could be coming soon wherein something truly horrific happens to young Mrs. Trent. And all of her advanced knowledge of quantum mechanics won't be enough to save her!"

Harper pursed his lips and leaned into Jeff.

"What kind of mechanic? Because, I gotta tell you, I'm looking for a guy. My Packard has been giving me trouble to no end lately."

Jeff ignored that, his fury turning on Eros.

"You *space bastard*! You think you can use my own wife against me? As a bargaining chip for me to sell out the human race?!?"

Tanna and Eros exchanged a look and shrugged.

"I mean, yeah, honestly. Kinda makes sense, don't you think?" Eros replied.

Without thinking, Jeff's fists curled into tight balls. He could feel his body coiling like a snake. Or the various silk ropes he kept neatly put away in his locker at the airport.

Those came in handy a lot. Just ask Danny.

"If you think I'm going to stand idly by while you use my wife for god knows what evil purpose, you're out of your space-bastard minds!" Jeff said, rage boiling under every syllable.

"We don't care what you do, human," Eros sneered. "You can't possibly stop us now!"

"We'll see about that!" Jeff declared, launching himself at

Eros, the two of them tumbling over the computer consoles, which blinked and winked like a Las Vegas showgirl.

Tom looked to Harper.

"Should we do something?"

Harper shrugged.

"Like what?"

Meanwhile, Kelton and Larry followed after Clay and Paula. For a bigger-framed person, Clay, even undead, was surprisingly nimble.

This seems as good a time as any to mention this:

There had been a rumor, when Clay had first joined the force, that he had a past in professional sports. He was so graceful for his size, it was hard to believe he hadn't had training in some form of athletics. In point of fact, one of the junior officers had done some digging, and had uncovered some evidence to suggest that Inspector Daniel Clay had, at one time, been better known as Giganto the Human Blimp, former Professional Wrestling Champion of the World for 1954.

Giganto had only briefly held the belt, about three months, before losing it to Handsome Hank Hartenraft, but he had made (if you'll pardon the pun) a big impression. He wore a bright red mask, and no one had ever seen him without it. But Giganto was known for his high-flying moves off the top rope to finish off his opponents. His infamous finisher was called, perhaps a little distastefully, 'The Hindenburg,' wherein Giganto would flip *backwards* off the top rope, do a complete somersault in mid-air, and land, belly first, right on his opponent's chest.

It was said that *no one* could recover from The Hindenburg, given the velocity, angle, and the sheer force of its impact. And scripted or not (and there were many of those who insisted that wrestling was as real as boxing, baseball, and badminton), Giganto, when he landed, landed *hard*.

Irony, however, is a cruel mistress, who comes and goes as she pleases. And in what turned out to be the final match of Giganto (against Handsome Hank), he went for The Hindenburg, but one of the more passionate fans of Hank threw his beer at Giganto, hitting him square in the face as he was about to flip, throwing off his balance and his sense of up and down. Giganto lost his positioning in space and landed awkwardly on his face instead of his belly, missing Hank entirely.

Hank, seeing the damage was real, quickly acted, rolling Giganto over onto his back and pinned him for the win and the title.

After exiting the ring, Hank (real name: Morrie Sheinberg from Yonkers) quickly called for an ambulance. It took six medics and Hank himself to get Giganto into the bus. One of those orderlies attempted to take off Giganto's mask, only to meet with an iron grip on his wrist.

"N—no," Giganto sputtered out. "Giganto must... must *never* be known!"

Hank shook his head in admiration. A professional to the last.

The ambulance raced off into the night, sirens wailing, red lights flashing into the dark. It was the last anyone had ever seen of Giganto the Human Blimp.

A couple of years later, a man of roughly Giganto's height and build showed up at the Burbank Police Department, with transfer papers from the San Diego Police Department, saying he was looking for a change of pace.

Now, that on its own merit wouldn't have meant much of anything, but it turned out that the wrestling promotion that Giganto was part of, Pink Valley Wrestling, was *based* out of San Diego.

Coincidence?

Could be.

But more than half the Burbank force was convinced that their own Inspector Clay was none other than former champion Giganto.

No one ever asked Clay about it. For one thing, they wanted to respect his privacy. For another, it was more fun to speculate and gossip.

At this moment, as the undead Clay shuddered and tumbled his way through the cemetery, Paula in his arms, Kelton was reminded of that Giganto rumor… and wondered if it had been true all this time.

"That son-of-a-bitch can *hustle*," Larry said, panting to keep up.

"As long as he doesn't perform one of his moves, we should be all right," Kelton muttered.

"What?"

"Nothing, nothing," Kelton countered. "C'mon! We gotta save Mrs. Trent, or there'll be hell to pay!"

The two cops plunged after Clay, racing to catch them before it was too late.

Paula Trent wasn't as unconscious as she seemed. After being grabbed by Clay and losing her senses briefly, she slowly came to, keeping her eyes closed, so as to feign helplessness.

But in fact, what she was *really* doing was collecting information, about where she was, where she was going, and the capabilities of the creature that held her in its arms. And soon enough, she had a plan.

It seemed that, despite its obvious strength and mindless, relentless *purpose*, this creature holding her still retained a couple of human characteristics. Namely, *balance*. It had to maintain its balance as it lumbered along, carrying Paula to who knew where. That was the point at which Paula would strike.

Slowly uncurling her fingers, she waited, counting the steps the beast took, finding a pattern. It was *lurch, lurch, lurch, lurch,* shuffle, *lurch, lurch, lurch...*

She waited for the next shuffle step and then...

Twisting around in the thing's tree-like arms, Paula raised her arms, and swiftly clapped her hands on each side of its head, right on the ears, boxing them.

There was a tremendous CLAP sound, and the creature stumbled from the effect.

Without hesitating, Paula boxed its ears *again*, using all the force she could muster.

The beast roared like a wounded lion, but still held his grip. So once more, Paula Trent, former captain of her intramural all-female rugby squad, *whacked* her strong hands against the ears of the zombie thug holding her.

Third time's the charm, so they say. And thus it was here.

The Clay Thing stumbled, groaning, swaying like a ship in a storm. Its eyes rolled back up into its head, and it fell, like a dead redwood, with a *BOOM* on the ground.

Paula, using her extensive gymnastics training, nimbly rolled herself out of the way and popped up, arms raised in triumph.

Kelton and Larry raced up just behind them, but screeched to a halt seeing the fallen former inspector.

"Whoa," Larry said, eyes wide. "Did you take care of that monster all by yourself, Mrs. Trent?"

Paula smirked, wiped her hands off, and nodded.

"I may be just a woman, boys, but I still know how to finish off a man."

Kelton thought about saying something in response to that particular phrasing, but decided it wasn't worth it in the end.

"C'mon," Paula said with authority. "Let's go help the others."

And with that, she dashed off in a straight line, having

already done the calculations to determine the most likely line of trajectory that Clay had been on.

"You heard the lady," Kelton said. "Let's go!"

He and Larry raced off, following the trail that Paula left behind. (She was a champion cross-country runner, so it was hard to keep up with her.)

Jeff and Eros were still rolling around the deck of the ship, grappling with each other.

It had been going on for a long time.

Tom turned to Harper.

"I think we should break this up. Don't you?"

Harper shrugged. He was eating popcorn that he had somehow found on the ship.

"I dunno. This is pretty good!"

"Where did you even get that?" Tom said, amazed, reaching for the popcorn, only to have Harper slap his hand away.

Suddenly, Tanna appeared from the depths of the saucer, menace on her face and a ray gun in her hand.

Harper was so struck by her, he dropped his popcorn.

"Well, take a look at that."

"Eros!" she barked out. "Stop fooling around with that human! More of their forces are on their way, and we have to get out of here!"

"I'm—not—fooling—around!" Eros struggled to say as Jeff gave him noogies on the top of his head. "I'm proving the superiority of the Klezmer people!"

"I don't really think you are," Tanna said, dry as a bone.

"Not… helping… Tanna!"

Tanna rushed over towards the flight controls.

"I'm getting us off this mudball of a planet, *now!*" she

declared, activating the engines. Tom and Harper looked at each other with alarm.

"They're heading into space! We have to get out of here before it's too late!" Tom shouted.

"Why are you shouting? I'm right here," Harper replied, holding his ears gingerly.

"Right, sorry."

The two men rushed for the door panels. They hit buttons randomly, not really understanding the technology (at one point they must have turned on a music feature because upright, sorta jazz-type sounds come gurgling out of the ship's speakers. Sorta sounded like something familiar to Edwards, but he couldn't quite place it).

The ship started rising off the earth slowly, as its anti-gravity thrusters kicked on.

"Goddamnit, Trent," Tom barked out, "Stop fooling around with that guy and help us! We gotta get out of here and quick!"

Jeff nodded and hauled back with his left fist and CLOCKED Eros right across the face, knocking him out!

"Take that, you space bastard," Jeff muttered as he climbed to his feet.

Tom finally managed to hit the correct combination of buttons on the door, and it slid open! "Let's get going while the going is good to go!" Harper said, rather convolutedly.

He dove through the open door, with Tom (after offering a quick little time-step) following right on his heels.

Jeff scrambled for the door, as the ship lurched further into the air.

"You'll never take over humanity," Jeff said defiantly, "we're too stubborn for that!"

He grabbed one of the desk chairs and hurled it across the room, hitting one of the computer stations and sparking a fire!

"Burn, baby, burn!" he said, a touch too gleefully and leapt out of the door, falling about seven feet to the earth below. Luckily, Jeff had taken far greater hits in his time and knew how to roll with it.

Tanna struggled with the flight controls as she careened the wobbling vessel into the upper atmosphere, and shutting the door to prevent oxygen loss.

Eros was unconscious, his body sliding back and forth like a pinball, hitting off walls and consoles, and all over the ship's deck as it took off into space.

(It was possible that Tanna rocked the ship back and forth a bit to induce further banging by Eros, but she would neither confirm nor deny that, when confronted with the flight recorder evidence during the investigatory council that was convened several weeks later on Klezmer.)

From the ground, it seemed as though the ship was engulfed in flame.

"Would you look at that?" Kelton said, just as he, Larry, and Paula arrived to find Tom, Harper, and Jeff all staring up at the sky.

As the six humans watched, the Klezmer spacecraft seemingly BURST into a massive explosion, sparks, lights, and debris all showered down from thousands of feet above, like fireworks on the Fourth of July.

At that moment, the Ghoul Woman, who had been wandering utterly lost in the cemetery and hadn't been used in this final sequence really at all, suddenly collapsed, reduced to bones and black fabric.

And the Clay Thing *also* turned from fleshy beast to skeletal figure (albeit a BIG one) in seconds.

The threat of the undead was over.

Meanwhile the human witnesses stood silently a moment, the fires in the sky lighting their faces like candles in the dark.

These half-dozen representatives of mankind had experienced something so unique, so strange, so life-altering, there were no words that could adequately describe it.

But that doesn't mean that they couldn't give it a try.

"We are not alone!" Larry Larry said, with fear and wonder.

"Space is the place!" Kelton said, proud of his rhyming scheme.

"To dream is to live!" Harper said, really not sure why.

"Leather weather is better weather!" Jeff inexplicably said.

"And woman shall inherit the earth," Paula said, with a quiet confidence that Jeff couldn't help but catch.

But it was trusty Colonel Tom Edwards that captured the moment, more so than any of them.

"We gotta hand it to them, though," he said thoughtfully, "they're far ahead of us."

EPILOGUE

Eros and Tanna survived the "explosion." It was standard Klezmer military procedure to cover any retreat with a diversionary tactic, in this instance, igniting the ship's trash to mask their escape.

The pair never returned to Earth. Indeed, they never worked together again.

Promptly upon their return to the station, and then on to Klezmer Prime, an investigation was launched regarding their mission, how the pair handled the execution of Plan 9 and the fallout resulting from said execution.

It didn't go well.

Both were *severely* reprimanded for the perceived failure of the mission and were given the option of reduced ranks and smaller duties, along with several rounds of public shaming.

More on Tanna and Eros in a moment.

Things for The Ruler, however, were a little more... strident, let us say.

Despite his title, The Ruler was, in fact, an elected position. And even though he'd held that position for many cycles, after the bungling of the whole Earth debacle, he was quickly removed from office in a vote of *'no confidence.'*

Disgraced, but unbowed, he wrote his (very) extensive memoirs, *The Rules of Engagement*, which became a runaway best-seller. But when the film version of the memoir was scheduled to be made, which was widely-anticipated, with pre-sales through the roof, The Ruler made a single demand: He simply *insisted* that he play himself, although he had no experience or training as an actor of any kind, on any level.

Not even a school play.

Let us say that was a poor casting decision.

The film flopped colossally, with the Klezmer cultural press skewering him relentlessly, calling his performance 'wooden', 'amateurish' and, perhaps, most damningly, 'setting back the craft of acting some thousand years into the past.'

Rough stuff, if, on the whole, accurate.

This sent The Ruler spiraling into a deep depression. But a Klezmer of such mettle couldn't be held down for long. And when he started designing rulers for use exclusively in an… *adult* manner, he finally found the place he was supposed to be in, even if that place still required him to sit down *gingerly*.

As for Tanna, after the investigation concluded, she retired from the Klezmer Space Forces permanently, having had enough adventure for a lifetime. She took her pension and finally lived up to that dream: Become an intergalactically recognized cooking show personality.

Her life became a whirlwind of personal appearances, book signings, talk-show guest spots, misbegotten romances with various celebrities, athletes, and politicians, but she always came back to her roots as the foremost colloquial chef in the known universe. But it was her speciality of marshmallows in a semi-frozen, fruit-based gelatin product that she had seen in a catalogue during her time on Earth that made her an absolute *star*. Intelligent species of all kinds just couldn't get enough of the stuff.

She called it *Eros' Secret* and there was speculation about: One—who Eros was; and two—what the secret was. Folks had their suspicions, as the marshmallows had a certain anatomical shape to them, but Tanna refused to answer such questions. She would just smile mysteriously and pivot the conversation back to the best uses of buttercream.

It was a good life.

Eros, meanwhile, following what was widely viewed as the abject failure of his mission, also chose to leave the military service rather than face demotion. Unfortunately, his next path was considerably less glamorous than that of his former colleague.

Word was he had moved out into the deep forests on planet Klezmer, leading a bit of hermetic existence, seeing few people and communicating even less with the outside world.

Until...

A thick package arrived in the inbox of the most prominent Klezmer newspaper, *The Daily Klez*, known for its hard-hitting journalism and take-no-prisoners style of writing.

The *Klez* was famous for taking the Klezmer government on with clear reporting, strong editorials, and political cartoons that, frankly, were utterly devastating.

This package included a heavily-researched, if poorly edited, account of Klezmer military attempts to eliminate potential threats to Klezmer life, through a series of "plans" that at least went up to nine, but rumor was there were as many *twelve* such plans, all without public input or knowledge, and with funding coming from—let us say—mysterious sources.

This document caused an absolute uproar in Klezmer society, creating an appetite for reforms in the armed services and governmental oversight. Known as "The Earth Epistles," this report became a cornerstone of modern Klezmer history and was credited with generating a total societal change for Klezmers everywhere.

The author of these epistles was never revealed, although many had searched and investigated the possibilities. It was generally agreed upon that this would go down as one of the great mysteries in Klezmer history, with no solution in the offing, even after decades of speculation.

However—

—there was one young intrepid Klezmer reporter who, somehow, had managed to track down the original envelope the document had arrived in.

There was no return address, but the postmark was from a mail station on the farthest edge of Klezmer civilization, an outpost for the most brave (and some would say *foolhardy*) of the population. It was right on the edge of civilization. There were only a few people known to live out there in the wilderness, scraping out a rough life, but an honest one.

That reporter heard rumors that a once-decorated Klezmer officer had built himself a home somewhere in those thick woods, only to be glimpsed occasionally as he came into town for supplies. But no one knew *exactly* where he lived out there.

His name was said to be Eros. It was also said, he could type like a son-of-a-bitch.

As for Jeff Trent...

Well. Following the events of Plan 9 and the Klezmer assault on Earth, Jeff decided to embrace that part of himself that has always been there.

He became a custom, home-wear leather craftsman. It wasn't easy, leaving the pilot life behind. There were plenty of nights when he would toss and turn, wondering if he had made the right decision.

But then he would feel himself nestled in his home-made leather harness, cradling him tightly from the ceiling, and he would breathe easier. *This* was where he belonged. Not hot-dogging it across the sky, but lurking in the dungeons of Burbank (which, coincidentally was what he called his business: *Trent's Dungeon Wear of Burbank*). The business boomed, partially because of the care and craft that Jeff took with his work—the human saddles were particularly popular—but also because of the *discretion* Jeff afforded all of his clientele. They ranged from ordinary, everyday folks to celebrities so famous that to name them would be to shake the American way of life to its core.

Jeff was *so* forward-thinking that he even went in early on using plant-based materials to create leatherwear for the environmentally-conscious and those in favor of animal rights.

That type of consideration made his business grow even bigger and eventually, he had no choice but to franchise the Dungeon. Soon enough, there were Dungeons Of Topeka, Allentown, Des Moines and Brisbane (although Jeff put a moratorium on using kangaroo leather. He just didn't think that was right).

More than anything else, his experience with the Klezmers had opened Jeff's eyes and mind to all possibilities that life could have.

With that in mind, he and Paula split. It was amiable and as caring as possible. He had come to understand that they had outgrown each other. It also wasn't anyone's fault. Sometimes, that was what happened in life. Aliens land and love changes. Who hadn't experienced that at one point or another?

Jeff found a leather queen who gave him everything he wanted out of his new life:

Respect for his work, honest criticism, and happily crating him most nights.

It was just right.

But...there were evenings when Jeff, leather gag in, stuffed into his crate, would crane his neck to try and see a sliver of the night from the window he could just make out from the angle he was in. And sometimes, there'd be a streak across the sky, and he'd wonder where that streak was going.

And if Paula could see it too.

Paula likely *did* see it. After the incidents over those few days, she decided that she was going to retire from all of her other work and focus exclusively on astronomy, physics, and the growing fields of aerodynamics in space travel.

She spent so much time at her telescope (which she helped design and build) up in the Cascade Mountains, that she became known as the "Lady on the Hill," a scientific figure of almost mythic reputation amongst the Western research community.

Graduate students, government researchers, private contractors—they all came from miles and miles away to consult with her, discussing the latest in rocket engineering, quantum string theory, and how to bake a mean banana bread in zero gravity.

Paula would demurely admit, if asked, that she enjoyed this newfound position of respect. It still felt awkward, what with her being a woman and all, but she figured that if other people found her useful, then, goshdarnit, she must be.

Indeed, she was *more* than just useful.

Paula became absolutely *essential* to the Space Race against the Soviets. She developed new satellite technologies that became the standard for all American launches. And what's more—Paula willingly volunteered to be the test pilot for all new aircraft designed to take to the heavens, putting her body through unimaginable hardships. After all her years of training as a mountaineer, she was the best candidate by far to handle the stresses of the g-forces and other physical strains put on the human body in such work.

Although denied the opportunity for first space flight, because, after all, she was only a woman, Paula was known colloquially as the "Godmother of Astronauts" because of her work, and was highly regarded amongst the new members of the Air Force and the newly created National Aeronautics and Space Administration.

She also was deeply *feared* on the other side of the Iron Curtain (at least in part because of several successful assassinations of high-ranking Soviet politburo members that had been attributed to her) because of her definitive work in the Space Race.

But, humble as always, Paula refused to take credit. It just wasn't her way. Even an alien invasion wasn't going to change that.

As for love? Well. That wasn't much of a concern for Paula these days. After she and Jeff had split, she resolved to "work on herself," feeling like she hadn't done enough yet to prove to herself that she belonged. Better to stay celibate for a spell. Get a handle on who she was now and mourn that which had passed.

And that resolution stuck...

...At least until Colonel Tom Edwards made his move.

After giving it some air, Tom click-clacked his way up to Paula's observatory, just as she was in the middle of some delicate research about folding space-time to create a new method of intergalactic travel.

Underachieving as always, Tom had said with a smile. Paula chuckled at that.

And then, with complete and utter earnestness, Tom

began to dance. Slowly at first, but with great expression and care. He had been working on this piece since learning that Paula and Jeff had split up.

The Klezmer incident had taught Tom that there really was no time like the present. And it was better to be bold than be safe.

Tom decided to be bold.

With the help of the principle dancer of the New York Ballet (who had started out as a tapper and owed Tom a favor after a misunderstanding involving the USO, a government contract, and six-hundred cartons of military-issue peanut butter), Tom choreographed a dance so intricate, so precise, that it took months of rehearsal.

Its goal?

To tell Paula the story of his love for her.

And boy, oh boy, did it work. Tom danced for the better part of three hours, complete with a string quartet, a brass quintet, and a woodwind septet (Tom liked the logical progression of numbered groups).

Paula was swept off her feet (literally. One of the movements of the dance involved a large broom), and she allowed herself to feel love again, a love that may have always been there, just under the surface.

And that love, now set free, *bloomed,* like the wildflowers that grew along the mountain where the observatory sat. Paula and Tom were soon married, a small ceremony, attended by a few of Tom's students, several of Paula's scientific colleagues, and the President of the United States. (He was a long-time fan of tapping and string theory, it turned out.)

With this new partner in the adventure of life, Tom decided to take another chance. He resigned his commission from the Army and opened a dance studio, right in the observatory.

Its polished stone floors were ideal for tapping and soon,

the school was full to bursting with dancers, all daring to dream just like Tom Edwards had, all those many years ago.

Larry Larry *did* change his name: to Rick Blaine. When someone pointed out to him that was the name of the Humphrey Bogart character in *Casablanca*, he changed it again, this time to Rhett Butler. And again, it was made clear that was the character Clark Gable played in *Gone with the Wind*. So, the third time must be the charm. He went with *Han Solo*. It worked, for a number of years at least, but because Larry never copyrighted that name, when a young filmmaker from USC made a movie with a character of the same moniker, he found himself in rough legal waters.

Larry tried to sue, but his attorney (found in the Yellow Pages, as they were the only attorney Han Solo—nee Larry Larry—could afford) told him he simply didn't have the resources to take on the filmmaker. As a result, *Han Solo* went back to being plain ol' Larry Larry.

It was, at first, a bitter pill to swallow. But in his later years, Larry found some solace in the teachings of various Hindi gurus, and soon, began *his own* teachings, preaching that serenity can be found in the embracing of the *self*, starting with one's own name.

As the decades wore on, and self-help became more and more popular, Larry Larry found himself in a position even better than that of a game show announcer:

Mental-health mentor.

It was the part he was born to play. By the time Larry Larry shuffled off this mortal coil, he was worth several million dollars, and with thousands of followers.

Go figure.

As for Kelton... well. Here's where things get a little... *strange*.

When the "police action" was declared in Vietnam, Kelton, still young enough, re-enlisted to "fight the Commies" as he told anyone that would listen.

Truth was, he was looking for some direction. After the Klezmer incident, Kelton thought his career would skyrocket, but in truth, it proved to be such a touchy subject that anyone directly involved in the whole affair was subsequently pushed out, hushed up, or promoted in return for silence.

Kelton wasn't important enough for any of those options, so he was left to stagnate. Those days got pretty hard; an endless loop of booze, whores, drugs, and circus peanuts. Kelton knew that if he didn't change and change *quick*, he'd be deader than an undead Clay.

Thus, when the Tonkin Gulf Incident occurred, it was almost a blessing.

So it was the army life for him.

Kelton shipped out to Vietnam, September 1st, 1964. He thought he'd be leading a platoon or maybe working for the military police, given his experience.

But that was not what happened. Instead, he was (disappointedly) made a private and sent off into the field like any other grunt.

Then, while out on a fairly standard patrol deep into the Vietnamese countryside, Kelton stopped for a moment to tie his shoes.

And that's all it took.

Looking up from his boots, there was no patrol, no voices, no *nothing* to tell him where he was or where his squad had gone.

He was lost.

(Kelton was terrible at navigation. Why do you think he could never find his way around that cemetery?)

Despite calling out for his fellow soldiers, there was no reply. (Kelton had suspected that maybe they ditched him, tired of hearing about the "aliens.")

He tried the compass, but as he didn't really know: A—what direction he had come from; B—what direction he was supposed to be going; or C—where the base was—it was of no use. He tossed it into the trees, where presumably it still lies to this very day.

He wandered through the jungles of southeast Asia for days, maybe weeks, surviving off rainwater and whatever fruit he could find.

As he sweated through his uniform and endured the stinging bites of insects the likes of which he had never seen, his mind started to swirl. Reality lost its focus, and it was as if he was traveling through another dimension.

He stumbled and tumbled through the thick forests of Vietnam, without seeing another human being. It got to the point where he was *certain* madness was descending upon him.

It started to rain—sheets, buckets of rain, absolutely torrential. Somehow, it got even hotter as a result.

Weak from exhaustion and dizzy from dehydration, Kelton collapsed, thinking he'd never missed the inside of the Burbank police station so much. As his eyes closed, he was certain he'd reached the end of his path.

And who knows? If he had fallen short a few steps, he may have.

Instead, a few days later, Kelton's eyes fluttered open, to a cool breeze and the sounds of wind chimes gently tinkling in his ears. He sat upright, to find himself deep within the cool recesses of a stone temple, ancient and holy, the soft scents of myrrh and incense burning.

As he found his footing, Kelton realized he was surrounded by monks, of what denomination, he couldn't say.

They were silent, sitting, legs folded, hands at rest, eyes closed, mediating.

And to Kelton's amazement—as one—they all floated off the stone floor, bobbing like corks on the ocean.

He had inadvertently found himself amongst the fabled Lost Monks of the Lotus. Priests, teachers, and mystics who believed that with study, silence, and generous doses of native psychedelics derived from local lotus flowers, humankind could truly achieve a transcendence from this plane of reality into something far, far greater. Something much more than what the crude frame of earthly flesh could contain.

Did Kelton himself find that transcendence?

Impossible to know, pointless to guess.

Although, in the deep villages of that part of the world, there were rumors of a Western man who came to a position of prominence amongst the monks. It was rumored he had even *achieved* that fabled promise of their beliefs.

It could never be confirmed.

Because Jack Kelton, former Burbank police officer, former private in the United States Army, survivor of the first alien invasion of Earth, was never seen on this world again.

And what happened to Lieutenant Harper, you may ask? After the events of the alien incursion, and after several reports detailing his leadership and bravery (submitted by the various officers, technicians, and patrolmen who were on site fro those strange few days), he was promoted to captain.

He missed the fieldwork, if he was being honest. But he didn't mind the bump in salary. Turned out Harper was good at command and promotions kept coming his way as his career continued, eventually going so far to become the commandant of the greater Los Angeles Police Academy.

By that time, the stories about the spaceships had become something like urban legend, as so many of the players directly involved with the incident had moved on or, as mentioned above, had vanished entirely.

Whenever a new class of police cadets came through, the rumors about flying saucers and zombie monsters inevitably spread like wildfire through the ranks. And Harper's name would, of course, come up.

Like clockwork, some brave young soul would eventually muster up the courage to approach Commandant Harper and ask about those stories.

"Word is you know something about… about *aliens*, sir…" the question would begin. "Is that true?"

That young cadet's eyes would be wide with fear and wonder and Harper would ruefully shake his head.

It was nearly a tradition at this point for someone to ask him.

But, under governmental restrictions not to speak about it, and frankly not wanting the headache on its own merit, Harper would just chuckle and shake his head.

"Just stories, son," he'd say, putting a hand on the student's shoulder. "Just rumors about the old man. There's no such thing as flying saucers, or space rays, or aliens from another world. Besides, we've got enough problems right here on Earth without worrying about what they're doing somewhere else, am I right?"

The student would nod, disappointed and perhaps relieved, racing back to his fellows to confirm that none of the stories were true.

But—

—if the student had managed to make a good impression, whether through politeness, respect, how snappy the uniform was kept, etcetera, that student might get a little surprise at the end of Harper's speech:

A quick, little wink.

Now, unfortunately, one of those winks was grossly misinterpreted and Harper found himself the object of obsession of one of these cadets. It got so bad, in fact, that Harper was forced to take early retirement, change his name, and move to the other side of the country.

Never having been to the East Coast, he decided that New York was the place for him.

However, Manhattan proved to be a bit too much. It was like L.A., but squeezed together more tightly. After decades of city-living, Harper (now known by a clever pseudonym that no one could possibly crack—*Hooper*) thought a little space was warranted and traveled up the Hudson River towards the Catskills, home of relaxing resorts, calm lakewaters, and thick trees to take a walk in.

He got a job working at a night club named *The Little Snitch*. Harper/Hooper assumed that it had something to do with organized crime, but the owner of the club, one Theros Smeros, (who was also one of its main attractions) told him it was actually an Americanization of a native word in his own tongue: *Litlesnitch*, which, Harper/Hooper was told, meant *music*.

What that native tongue *was* exactly, Harper/Hooper could never find out. He presumed it was somewhere in Eastern Europe. God knows all those poor bastards had a tough time with the Soviet Reds out that way. But whenever he would ask about Theros' homeland, Theros would just smile, shake his head and say, *You'd never believe me if I told you.*

He'd then bound up on stage with his family, about twelve of them, and play the most rip-roaring, yet oddly low-key, music you'd ever heard. Folks traveled up from the city all the time to see them. (*Lots* of folks from Eastern Europe, Harper/Hooper would notice).

After being at the club for a couple of weeks, Harper/Hooper found he really enjoyed listening to the band rehearse. He just couldn't get enough of it.

During one such rehearsal, as Theros stepped offstage for a break, Harper/Hooper approached him.

"Boss," he said, "You know, we didn't get music like this out in Los Angeles. It was all that rock n' roll stuff. Not for me, if I'm being honest. But this? Man, it speaks right to my soul. What do you call it?"

Theros took a moment before answering, looking right into Harper/Hooper's eyes with intensity and a knowing smile.

"We call it… *Klezmer* music."

Harper/Hooper's eyes grew wide at the recognition of that name.

"Wait, do you mean… are you—"

Theros put a finger to his lips, silencing Harper/Hooper before he could finish.

"Come with me, my friend," Theros said mysteriously. "And I'll answer all the questions you have, about so many other things."

The exact details of that conversation have never been revealed, but it seemed that Harper/Hooper did indeed get the answers to at least *some* of those questions. Regardless, he was never happier in his life than during his time at *The Little Snitch*.

He became such an advocate for Klezmer music and the message it offered that he himself became synonymous with the music, becoming as welcome a fixture at the club as the musicians themselves.

Time passed and passed well.

So it was that when Harper/Hooper finally died, some thirty years later, he was the last surviving human who had direct contact with those events of late 1957, when for a brief moment, mankind understood that they were not alone.

Theros was there, at his bedside, not having aged a day (as we know, Klezmers age at a much slower rate than humans do. Theros kept pretending to be his own son as the years went by), holding Harper/Hooper's hand, while the rest of the band softly played *Hey, Tsigelekh*, his personal favorite.

"Don't be afraid," Theros said, the music chiming lightly in Harper/Hooper's ears. "You're about to witness something more glorious than you could ever possibly imagine."

"But...but will you–"

Theros reached out and caressed Harper/Hooper's face with a gentle touch.

"We'll see you there, one day. Our old friend."

Reassured and satisfied, Harper/Hooper smiled, closed his eyes, and drifted away.

Thus passed into forgotten history the legend of Plan 9 from Outer Space, the plan that was meant to end humanity's threat to the universe, but instead, it elevated at least *one* human being's place from this thin plane of existence, into something much larger, much more hopeful, something much more *joyous* than the one we found ourselves stranded in.

There are more things in heaven and earth... than are dreamt of in your philosophy, the great poet once said.

Harper/Hooper learned that to be true indeed. As did all of those souls who found themselves part of this strange story.

Perhaps there is a chance that will be true *of us all* as eternity stretches on.

And now... for a final question:

...Will such visitors come to us again?

Who can say?

But we can *hope*, dear friends, that if and when they do, we may be better equipped to deal with them. Talk with them. *Commune* with them. At least, more than we were in the middle part of the twentieth century.

Thank *you*, gentle readers, for joining me on this strange, miraculous, foolhardy, breathtaking, confusing, cheaply-filmed, but endearingly ambitious, tale.

By the way, in case you've been curious all this time…

…I have been… Criswell. Your narrator through this most singular of adventures.

And I bid you…

Farewell.

<u>THE END...?</u>

THIS BOOK

Famously dubbed "the worst film ever made" in 1980, by film critics Harry and Michael Medved, **Plan 9 from Outer Space** has become the lasting legacy of Ed Wood—who was also named "the worst director of all time" at the Golden Turkey Awards (also in 1980).

The film is also notable for a few other reasons:

1) Star Gregory Walcott later became best friends with Clint Eastwood.

2) It's the incidental second act in what's been called "The Kelton Trilogy." Wood's previous film, **Bride of the Monster**, and his next film, **Night of the Ghouls**, also featured the hapless patrolman.

3) Perhaps importantly, it is the final film of Bela Lugosi. It should be said that, at this time, Lugosi was unable to find work, struggling with drug addiction and considered washed-up. Wood helped Lugosi through his addiction and his depression, and gave him his last few roles, giving the horror icon something to work towards. While some (including Lugosi's son) dispute the notion that Wood was entirely altruistic in his motives, many others (as quoted in *Nightmare of Ecstasy*, Wood's biography) say the friendship was genuine. Regardless, in a roundabout way, Wood achieved what he set out to do as a filmmaker:

Find immortality.

Cast:

Jeff Trent **Gregory Walcott**
Paula Trent **Mona McKinnon**
Lieutenant John Harper **Duke Moore**
Colone Tom Edwards **Tom Keene**
Eros **Dudley Manlove**
Tanna **Joanna Lee**
The Ruler **John Breckinridge**
General Roberts **Lyle Talbot**
Patrolman Larry **Carl Anthony**
Patrolman Kelton **Paul Marco**
Danny **David De Mering**
Edie the Stewardess **Norma McCarty**
Farmer Calder **Karl Johnson**
Inspector Dan Clay **Tor Johnson**
Vampire Girl **Maila Nurmi (Vampira)**
Old Man/Ghoul Man **Bela Lugosi**

ACKNOWLEDGMENTS

Thanks to many, but especially:
    Dan Hodge
    Nick Jackson
    Cherry Weiner
    Christie Parker
    Ned Delaney
    Colin P. Delaney

—And Edward D Wood, Jr. (1924-1978)

ABOUT THE AUTHOR

Jared Michael Delaney is an author, stage/screen writer & actor based in Philadelphia Pa. His full length plays have been produced at Perseverance Theatre, New Jersey Repertory Company, Inis Nua Theatre Co, the Yes! Festival, Edinburgh Festival and Theatre Conspiracy. His short plays have been been part of the QuarenStream, 1MPF & Going Viral online festivals and others produced by Athena Theatre, NJ Rep, MadLab Theatre, Aberrant Theatre, Pegasus Theatre, Raze the Space and the Philadelphia LiveArts Festival. His work has been further presented at the Valdez Theatre Conference, Sewanee Writers' Conference, Middlebury Acting Company's New American Play Festival, among other readings across the country.

He's been a member of curated writers' groups Athena Writes and The Foundry. His play, *Voyager One*, was named a "Top Ten Production of the Year in New Jersey" in 2019. His screenplays have placed in such competitions as the Austin Film Festival, Big Break, Launch Pad, Screencraft and the Atlanta Film Festival. He is the co-host of a weekly podcast about the musician Prince, titled **When Doves Podcast**, available on all platforms.

His adaptation of the 1966 film **Billy The Kid Vs. Dracula** is also available from Cult Pulp Press.

M.A., Villanova University; M.F.A., Queens University of Charlotte. Member: Dramatists' Guild, AEA, SAG-AFTRA, New Play Exchange.

www.jaredmichaeldelaney.com

COMING ATTRACTIONS

Plan 9 From Outer Space by Dan Hodge

Messiah of Evil by Jared Michael Delaney

Horror Express by Dan Hodge

It! The Terror From Beyond Space by Jared Michael Delaney

Bluebeard by Dan Hodge